SHADOWS
AND
SHIMMER

SHADOWS
AND
SHIMMER

stories

PATRICK SEDA

TITAN SHORE PRESS
An Imprint of Saturn Moon Beach Productions

Titan Shore Press is an imprint of Saturn Moon Beach Productions

www.titanshorepress.com

FIRST EDITION

Cover design by Lance Buckley
Author photograph by Billy Kelly Photography

ISBN 979-8-218-11431-2

For my family.

Sprinkle the seeds of your dreams
far and wide.
For when they grow, they become
a path to anywhere.

CONTENTS

CONTENTS

SHADOWS
AND
SHIMMER

SHADOWS AND SHIMMER

I REMEMBER THE HOUSE, but for some reason, I remember the driveway more. Weeds lounged in the cracks and gaps and crumblings. It could barely pass for a solid surface anymore, but it was nonetheless still a driveway. A fallen branch from a giant oak rested on its elbow, propped up onto the weed-encroached fragments of concrete. A few of last autumn's leaves were still clinging to the intact smaller branches. In the front yard, the weathered *For Sale* sign sported a clean white *Sold* banner. Mr. Chapman had, apparently, committed to bringing the house back to life. I stood on the sidewalk and stabilized myself with my walking cane, noticing how dirty the windows were.

Mr. Chapman left me a message in the morning and described the situation in his new house. He begged for help. He emphasized his daughter's overwhelming fear and how he was certain he had had an aneurysm when lights seemed to glow from the inside of his eyes.

Now he waved toward the house and repeated some of the words from his earlier message, but I wasn't really listening. I chose not to. I knew I would find the problem—the stench gave it away. The stale effluvium had entered my nose the moment I arrived. It was always a musky blend of stink bug and cilantro.

That's what ghosts smell like.

I asked Mr. Chapman how long he'd been living here, how long he'd been having the problem. He bought the house two weeks prior and started moving furniture the previous weekend. His family had only stayed two nights but now were too frightened to attempt another.

"I've heard about this house," I said.

I SOMETIMES CHAT WITH MRS. EVANS over coffee in the library lobby cafe. Our husbands were lifelong friends but recently she became a widow too, so now our frequent chats help with the loneliness.

She mentioned a house, not too far from the library, that the owners insisted was clean one day and haunted the next. They refused to stay any longer so they rented it out for a while. Every subsequent tenant had the encounter and scorned the lease. The owners finally decided to sell, but a house with such a reputation invariably sat unoccupied for two years.

"EVERYONE ALWAYS SEES IT," I said.

Mr. Chapman's face washed pale, "Everybody knows?"

"I can help," I said as I thrust my cane outward to start a slow shuffle. My legs carried my wobbly hitch toward the front door. My energy isn't what it used to be, but I had an immutable agenda to assay houses like these.

As I stepped through the front door I could see movement in the kitchen. Some people have the occasional ability to see ghosts, children more than adults. Sometimes it's a vague movement in the peripheral vision, sometimes it's the drifting and dancing lights. But I myself see a ghost in its full representation. I see the mist that flows through the cracks and gaps in the fault line between the living and the afterlife. Flowing, yet solid. Sadness, yet intention. Lounging, yet urgent.

Mr. Chapman's ghost was pacing in the kitchen. I stepped

into the doorway and waited. She paced near the sink and kept pausing at the window, craning her neck to look out onto the driveway. She seemed to be looking for something specific through that dirty window. I doubt she cared about the weeds and crumbling concrete, and I doubt she cared about the fallen oak branch. I waited and watched.

REGARDLESS OF RECEIVING CALLS to help rid homes of ghosts, I prefer to think of my usefulness as helping ghosts release themselves from homes. I don't know why some people become ghosts. I don't know why they resist passing over. But they're always confused about what is happening to them, confused about the flowing mist that used to be the memories of their lives.

MR. CHAPMAN'S GHOST KEPT PACING at the sink and looking out the window. I continued to wait in silence. At one point she stopped pacing and brought her hand to her cheek, "Oh dear!" she said in a phasing whisper and ran toward the closed back door and disappeared. That was when she released her shimmer, the moment she left the air sparkling like a moonrise over a calm sea.

"You have a Shimmer," I said to Mr. Chapman, "but it's gone now."

"It's gone? ... for good?"

"No."

"Can't you get rid of it? I was hoping—that's what you do, right?"

It's always the same question.

"No," I said, "I can't get rid of a Shimmer, but you can."

Mr. Chapman showed the same confusion my words always produce. They ask. I answer. Then the confusion.

"Your Shimmer is bound to this kitchen. Shimmer can move around but they only inhabit a specific area and stay within it, very small areas that had some importance in their life. Maybe it was their childhood home, maybe a party they went to, or perhaps ..."

"It's where they died?" Mr. Chapman interrupted.

I hesitated but decided not to finish my sentence. Most people assume a haunted locus is the place of death, but that's rarely the case. I checked my watch, "Perhaps," I said.

I waited for the Shimmer to return. She materialized soon afterward as her mist congealed near the sink and she started pacing again. Her behavior was rather limited—pacing and worrying—and it was clear she wasn't a threat to the family.

"It's a busy one," I said.

A less active Shimmer can go unnoticed for quite some time if their emotional pulse and light release happens when no one is around. But this one was quite active and had the unusual timing of shimmering itself as it passed through Mr. Chapman's head.

"Your Shimmer is bound to this space, this kitchen. You have to make it unrecognizable to their memory."

"Unrecognizable?"

"Change the space. The colors, the configuration—it will become confused and leave for good. The more you change, the better. There are never Shimmer in new houses."

Mr. Chapman described the remodeling he was planning. Cabinets, lighting, center island—I deemed it sufficient to make his Shimmer move on. I suggested he start immediately.

Trepidation crept into his voice, "Okay ... but what about my daughter's room?"

"Your Shimmer is confined to the kitchen, it cannot move to the bedroom."

"It's in her bedroom too—she's afraid to go in there."

I didn't want to believe him. This meant two ghosts, and two within such proximity to each other would be quite remarkable. But since a child had the encounter I couldn't dismiss it. His eyes didn't belie his daughter's fear. I was surprised I hadn't acknowledged the exaggerated ghost stench before this. In hindsight, it was much too strong to be just one—I should have known by the intensity as it hit my nose on the sidewalk. I wasn't done yet.

"What has she seen?" I asked.

"She says a cold shadow stares at her while she sleeps."

I asked if he was sure of it—he must be certain of these words. My tone was serious and firm. An immobile shadowy figure is different from a Shimmer, it behaves differently and must be addressed differently. He was describing a Shadow entity. In all of my experience, I've never seen a house to have both a Shimmer and a Shadow.

"Show me," I said.

Mr. Chapman led me to the short hallway and stopped at a closed door. He pointed as he crept backward, "There."

AT ONE LIBRARY VISIT WITH MRS. EVANS, when we were discussing the cafe's newest flavor of coffee, she asked me why I do it—why I keep cleaning houses when there's nothing in it for me.

"Hope," I told her.

AS I PUSHED OPEN THE DOOR, ghost stench and coldness wafted over me. I saw him. He stood beside an old dresser with his palm resting atop. The Shadow was clearly defined and radiated waves of dark blue mist from his flowing dark surface. Our eyes met. He carried a long sadness on his face. His eyes pleaded with me to acknowledge him.

"Mr. Chapman, let's talk in the hall," I said as I backed out of the room. I never broke my gaze with the Shadow, I wanted him to know I could see him.

I told Mr. Chapman that this was a different kind of ghost; this was a Shadow. And unlike Shimmer, these don't move around and don't respond to changing the space of the living. I explained that a Shadow is attached to some object—a bed, or hairbrush, or even something small like a coin—clinging to something associated with their death.

"How do we get rid of it?"

"The singular way to get rid of a Shadow is to destroy the object it is bound to."

"How do we know what the object is?"

I knew the answer to my question but asked anyway, "Is anything new in the room ... new to your possession?"

He told me that on their first day living in the house, his wife had purchased that old dresser at a garage sale. The sellers were ardent to get rid of it and even offered to just give it for free.

I explained that I was certain the Shadow's binding object was the old dresser itself. I described the way the ghost stood so close to it, the way his hand laid so possessively upon the top. I concluded the sellers at the garage sale probably knew something about it was wrong.

MRS. EVANS HAS KNOWN ABOUT my abilities for decades. She always understood my hesitation to try new places to meet for coffee. We settled on the cafe in the library lobby because it was remodeled a few years back and so far there's been no ghostly distractions there.

My husband understood my situation even better still. He had such an innocent heart for nostalgia and loved hunting antique tchotchkes from our childhood. Occasionally he would find something he loved and bring it home. "What do you think about this one?" he would ask with a big smile. He placed them all around the house. "For my future memory," he would say.

But I couldn't spend that time with him, those moments when his soul was filled with the most joy while browsing for sentimental reminders. Thrift stores are too noisy and too crowded for me—not with people, not with melange, but with Shadows and Shimmer.

I regret the day he passed. I regret that I wasn't with him. I wasn't there to lie to him and tell him everything would be all right. I wasn't there to hold his hand and caress his head. I selfishly wasn't in that thrift store because I was excessively tired of being around ghosts.

"SO WE HAVE TO DESTROY the dresser?"

"Yes, and quickly. It must be removed from such close proximity to the Shimmer in your kitchen. This could get bad if you don't."

"I suppose I could put it to the curb and cut it up."

"No. That is not the way. I will take care of it. My nephew will come—he has experience with Shadow removal."

Mr. Chapman and I made our way to the end of the driveway and I called my nephew. He arrived quickly and the two men loaded the dresser onto the truck.

After my nephew left, I couldn't help but contemplate the driveway. I saw where cracks had formed in the concrete and where gaps had expanded. I noticed where weeds had taken root, and where they had not. I wondered if ghosts, like weeds, were incapable of understanding their existence in a world where they weren't welcome.

THAT EVENING I SAT ON THE EDGE of my bed and smiled. It was a long, yet successful day. I thought of the relief on Mr. Chapman's face as he watched the dresser get carried away. I thought of how his family would soon be rid of their Shimmer too, and happier days would arrive. I thought about how Mr. Chapman will fix his home and fix his driveway and mend all the crumblings.

MY HUSBAND WAS BROWSING tchotchkes the day he passed, and for that I am grateful. He died with a heart full of joy. He became dizzy as the room spun out from under his feet. His head met the corner of old oak craftsmanship as he fell.

After laying my husband to rest, Mrs. Evans accompanied me to the shop where he had passed. The clerk was agreeable and showed me the spot where he had fallen. It was empty, but she showed me regardless. She also described how when they found him he was grasping the leg of an old dresser, his arm stretched out as if embracing that dresser was the most important thing he would ever do.

They could not show me the dresser, it had already been sold. I've been looking for it ever since because I've been looking for my husband. He understood that he was about to leave our world, that he had but one moment of life left. He also understood Shadows and how they bind to objects. He wasn't near one of his prepared tchotchkes at home, so he did the best he could.

My nephew had known that an urgent call to remove a dresser meant that I had finally found it, and the removal was not intended for destruction but was to end up in my bedroom, in the dresser-sized spot I had kept empty for many years.

HOPE. I WASN'T LYING WHEN I told Mrs. Evans I do it for hope. When I realized my husband was hoping to make himself into a Shadow, I filled with the hope that I would be able to find him. Now, every night when I sit on the edge of my bed, I smile. I smile at the dark blue mist radiating from the flowing surface of my husband.

And he smiles back.

THE SCARLET JOB

WITH THE ONSET OF GRIM NOVEMBER, the arctic tormentors of the north had sent their best warrior, powerful and cold and armed with ammunition to last well into February. A blanket of gray clouds rested upon the peaks of the city, tucked in tightly at the corners of the horizon. Diffused light crept around tenements and spilled into eyes mourning for the warmth of summer.

The evening streets of Chicago were slowing and the assured onset of stinging rain would soon grow and fold itself into sheets. The wind became strong and threw pulsing waves with attempts to reach under men's hats and grab their necks, only to be foiled by raised collars gripped in fervor.

New Studebakers and Chevrolets sped past parked Model Ts, spitting mud unto their drab and inferior finishes. Passing tires seared the wet pavement, a contemptuous reminder to the homes of the working class that expensive steaks were being served in white gloves just across the river.

TO ANGELO, THIS WAS MERELY a deferential business call to dispatch a commission. He dropped his cigarette into a puddle before moving up the stairs of the soot-stained brownstone.

The new kid had a name but everyone was calling him *Bones*—an understandable reference to his long and lanky build. Bones came with the reputation of an accurate shot so he stayed at the bottom of the stairs watching for approaching cars and adversaries of concern.

Angelo's physique was well-established and burly. An upturned coat collar wrapped his immense neck. An expensive hat sat low over his brow and the sideways rain kept trying to wet his two-day stubble. Angelo knuckled three polite taps on the door and fixed his eyes on the sidelight window.

Through the dark hallway, Angelo saw a light come on in the back room.

"He's here," Angelo announced to Bones.

"Good. My dogs are swimming."

"Keep your eyes on, kid."

The entryway illuminated and a small silhouetted man leaned to investigate the late visitor.

Angelo lifted his palm in muted greeting.

The man cupped his hands around his eyes and pressed against the window.

"Yes? It's very late!" his scratchy words muffled through the glass.

Angelo pulled back his lapel to show the man his holstered Colt.

The shadow jerked back before leaning against the window again to study the statuesque Bones under the sidewalk streetlamp. The man inspected Angelo up and down before a loud click unlocked the door.

"I'm sorry sir, it's quite late for a visit," the elderly man said while cracking open the door.

Angelo was a full foot taller and fifty years younger. The old man pressed his cheek against the edge of the door and gripped it with nervous fingers.

"I'm here for Mister Scarlet, I've got a job for him," Angelo said in a low rumble.

"Sir, you must have the wrong house, there is no Mister Scarlet here."

Angelo glared down with calm intimidating eyes.

"Mister Scarlet rooms at 447 Huron," Angelo said, "And I'm standing at 447 Huron. So I'd like to see him. Please."

"Well, yes sir, you stand on the steps of 447, but—but it's just me and my wife here. She's Dorothy and I'm Jacob—Kasper. Kasper is our name, not Scarlet."

Angelo spoke with an unwavering calm, "Invite me in from this miserable weather. Please."

Mister Kasper opened the door just enough for Angelo to enter and latched the door behind him.

"If you don't mind sir, would you shake your coat off over the entryway rug there? I wouldn't want anyone to slip."

Angelo brought both hands to his lapels and gave a firm snap—a fountain of water sprayed from his coat.

"So ... Scarlet, I'd like to see him," Angelo said.

"No disrespect, but as I said, it is only my wife and me in this tenement. We are Jacob and Dorothy Kasper. I will call her out if you wish."

Jacob leaned into the hallway and raised his voice, "Dear, please come to the front!"

"Who is it? Don't they know it's late?" a feeble voice called back.

"Dorothy, please!"

Floorboards creaked and Mrs. Kasper walked with an arthritic hitch toward the two men. She dried her hands on the upturned fabric of a pasta sauce-stained apron.

"Jacob, is this a friend?" she asked as she removed her reading glasses and tucked loose hair under her headscarf.

"This is my wife," Jacob said, "We are just cleaning up from supper. Dorothy, this is ..."

Jacob turned his palm to Angelo and hoped for an introduction.

"Ma'am, I've come to speak with Mister Scarlet, here on business."

"There's no Mister Scarlet here," Dorothy began, "It's only the two of us. Not even our children live here anymore."

"I was assured 447 Huron is where I find Scarlet. Mister Nitti sent me himself, said they're old friends. Can we get on with it? Please."

"I mean no disrespect, certainly not to—*oh my*, did you say Nitti? Frank Nitti sent you to our home? Oh, dear, Jacob—Frank Nitti," Dorothy said with nervous worry.

"Now calm down, Dorothy," Jacob said with his hands raised in assurance, "I'm sure there's a good explanation. We have no beef with Frank Nitti."

Just then the entryway telephone rang; all eyes turned.

"Who on earth could be calling at this ungodly hour?" Dorothy said before stepping to pick up the receiver, "What a preposterous night—I do say."

"Hello?" she said, "Hello mother. Be a dear and let me ring you back shortly, I have an unexpected guest ... okay mother."

Dorothy set the receiver down and turned a worried face toward the men. Angelo stood large and expressionless. Jacob's nervous eyes darted between the two.

"Mister ... uh ... Mister—" Jacob began, uncertain if he had heard his visitor's name, "We're just simple florists, we own Kasper Flowers over on Wells—surely you've seen it while driving along. Kasper Flowers, that's our shop, Jacob and Dorothy Kasper."

Angelo pursed his lips.

"You let rooms?" he rumbled.

"No," Jacob answered with certainty.

Angelo scanned the entryway and front room.

"Any guns in the house?"

"Most certainly not!" Dorothy responded, "We don't run with hoodlums, but we *do* arrange beautiful flowers for their frequent funerals."

Angelo stared stone-faced at Jacob and held an uncomfortably long silence. Then Angelo lifted one corner of his mouth and said, "You two don't look like killers to me anyhow."

"That's right, sir." Dorothy said, "I'm still confused how you could end up here for such an unseemly visit?"

"Nitti gave it to me directly—told me to bring the kid for cover."

Angelo tucked his tongue into his lower lip before straightening his collar.

"Sorry to bother, folks. I'll get this sorted, have a good night. And I've seen your shop—it's a good shop, you do good work."

Angelo opened the door and took a step out into the rain, but Bones wasn't at the bottom of the stairs. Angelo paused on the landing and tipped his head to look down the street. The wind persisted and the rain had increased and was beginning to reach under Angelo's hat and sting his face.

"Bones!" he called out, his booming voice fighting with the howling and rumbling weather.

"Bones!"

Angelo crept his hand upward inside his lapel, but before he reached his gun, a powder blast exploded next to his hip and another flashing gunshot cracked across the street as the thin silhouette of Bones fell into the gutter.

Angelo leaped sideways to find Dorothy kneeling beside him with a rifle pointed across the street. Angelo's eyes were wide as he franticly searched his torso for wounds.

Dorothy lowered her rifle and stood.

"Come back inside, Angelo," Jacob spoke with calm assurance.

Angelo scurried inside and Jacob closed the door.

"Are you okay, young man?" Dorothy asked.

"Yeah—yeah, all jake. What happened?"

"The kid was a plant from Bugs Moran," Dorothy began, "he was going to kill you on the steps tonight—the rain his assistant in cleaning away evidence ... to wash your blood into the sewer."

"Who are you two?"

"We haven't lied, we own the flower shop," Jacob answered.

Dorothy stepped over to the phone and picked up the receiver from the tabletop. She had failed to disconnect the earlier call and the receiver had been resting on its side.

"Angelo," she said as she held the receiver out to him.

Angelo crept toward Dorothy, his eyes still wide, and cradled the phone.

"Hello? ... Hello Mister Nitti. Yes—yes I'm fine. Bones is down. The woman, she ... thank you, sir."

Angelo handed the phone back to Dorothy and she hung up. Dorothy stepped in front of Angelo and cupped his giant hands into hers.

"You're valuable to Mister Capone, Angelo. Which means you're valuable to us."

Jacob rubbed a soapy cloth against Angelo's coat near his hip where Dorothy had fired.

"This tenement is a safe spot for you, as is our flower shop. If you're feeling heat, come by and ... shop for some flowers," Dorothy said with a wink.

She reached up and straightened Angelo's lapels and gave them a pat with her open palms.

"And by the way," Dorothy said, "it's *Miss* Scarlet."

SPLICES

EVERY MORNING BETWEEN SEVEN o'clock and nine, the corner booth belonged to four retired railroad welders. It was the prime real estate of the diner overlooking the corner of Thirteenth and Nichols. And in that booth, the men sipped coffee and gossiped and teased each other, all the while remaining firmly stuck in the past.

A standing rib was Richie accusing Little Hank that his bad welding of a rail yard splice caused the big freight train derailment of '98. The irony of it was that Little Hank, who was by far the largest of the men, was the best welder at the yard, and Richie, who was by far the smallest man, was severely farsighted and was only ever given the simplest repairs.

Phil's long ponytail and full beard were heavily streaked with gray, and not quite as intimidating as when they used to be a deep jet black. As far back as high school, he was called 'Phil the Pirate' for his sunken eyes and outlaw looks. Little Hank referred to Phil as 'Which One' and insisted he couldn't tell Phil apart from his wife, "Which one are you?" Little Hank would say. Phil insisted Richie was one of those little blind rats from the oat processing plant that wandered over and somehow got hired by accident.

Eddie was the forgettable one. His expressions were constrained to a minimal range of smiles and smirks. His wireframe glasses were conservative, yet never seemed to go out of style even as the decades passed. Eddie had become a bit softer around the middle over the years, his hair thinning. He was always the quiet, unremarkable one—but was perfectly content staying in the background. He had never been comfortable in the spotlight.

Exaggerations were common as the men spun their stories in the diner. Little Hank once claimed he was offered a full scholarship to play football at Nebraska, but turned it down because he didn't want to hurt all his friends who played for Iowa. Richie claimed he used to be a Navy SEAL, but his missions were so top secret he couldn't discuss them. Phil claimed he was secretly the famous Motown songwriter Moses Javelin who wrote under a fake name to keep mobbing fans away. Eddie claimed he had a bar of Hitler's gold at home and that his grandfather stole it from Hitler's bunker. Every day the men's stories created handfuls of air to be swatted toward each other.

The men loved classic cars. They spent every Saturday afternoon of the summer sitting in lawn chairs at an arm's distance from restored rods at the nearly-dead shopping mall. Little Hank teased Phil that his Olds would look cooler with more chrome on its boring black finish. Phil teased Richie that he probably should carry his mustard-stain Pinto around in a woman's purse. "Better close the zipper so it don't fall out and bump the gas tank— kaboom!" he would say. Eddie was secretly jealous of Little Hank's yellow deuce coupe, but could never in good conscience come to tease him about it. That yellow beauty always got the most attention and Eddie was glad to avoid the spotlight.

ANY OLD VEHICLE DRIVING around the diner corner past the welders was fair game for a condescending quip. If a car was old enough to be a classic, then there was—according to the men— no excuse for it not to be converted into a hot rod.

Except for Old Man Gorski's F150 pickup.

Or, more precisely, the one he *used* to own.

Mister Gorski purchased the truck the same month 'Jaws' was uncaged onto terrified beachgoers forty-some years before. The unblemished finish was the green of creamy pea soup, an avocado hue shared with kitchen appliances (that weren't the era's coppertone or harvest gold). The unfashionable whitewalls clung to stock rims, and hubcap crowns of chrome reflected a wide-angle view of blacktop and blue skies.

The men remembered those rare days when that truck sauntered around with Mister Gorski at the wheel. Rare indeed, because the telephone company had gifted him a roomy sedan along with his big promotion. "Better to wear down the company car instead of my own," he would say. He kept that truck in the garage where it remained washed, waxed, and frozen in time.

Ever since the loss of Mister Gorski, whenever the pristine green truck crept to a stop at Thirteenth and Nichols, the welders fell silent. No one spoke until the truck cleared the corner. But they all thought the same thing, *It don't seem right for that Mexican to be driving Gorski's truck.*

Phil was always first to respond with his trademark grunt, then Richie would comment on how Old Man Gorski wouldn't like this situation much at all. Little Hank would shake his head, inducing his double chin to wobble. Eddie never commented but always wondered why Gorski's wife would sell that beautiful truck to some stranger.

AUTUMN WAS BRISTLING with a crisp, cool breeze as the men left the diner one morning. Peak color was passing and the tiring trees had begun to release their leaves to be free and flutter. Richie casually mentioned that the lottery was at an all-time high but there was no way he was just going to throw away his money like some stupid fool. Phil and Little Hank laughed in support. Eddie remained silent.

A melancholy worry had been creeping into Eddie's chest. The four friends had retired from the railroad a year and a half prior, all having reached the mandatory retirement age of fifty-five. They had all become swept up in the growing excitement of *getting the hell out of there* and felt rebellious looking forward to the day they could hang up their coveralls and gloves and give a giant one-finger salute to the rail yard.

But Eddie had been thinking about his future, his legacy, and self-reflecting on what impact his life actually had on the world. The railroad would continue to need repairs and new kids would be hired to replace the disappearing old-timers. The welds and splices they bragged and teased about would one day be torn out. Eddie had planned his retirement finances with conservative responsibility, but the reality that his usefulness was expired left him uneasy. The goal line for the men had only been to get to retirement—to hit the end zone and spike the ball and dance in defiance. But not much thought had been given to the possibility of another twenty or thirty years of diminishing health. The lack of a meaningful legacy had saddled Eddie with thoughts of insignificance.

EDDIE LEFT THE DINER AND TOOK a different route home that day. He drove past the old courthouse and slowed to look at the two naval artillery cannons mounted on either side of the front steps—steadfast monuments to the first World War. Eddie thought about the young sailors who had once fired these cannons during the war, young and afraid and unfairly forgotten beneath a headstone now. He thought about how those magnificent guns were icons of an era of fear and uncertainty, an era that meant nothing to the mothers who scolded their small children for simply climbing on the cannons for fun.

Eddie parked in front of Willie's tire shop and gave Willie Jr. a wave through the display window. Reaching the crosswalk, Eddie noticed Gorski's green pickup parked around the corner.

It was rare to see the pickup in town, other than the occasional sighting at the diner corner. Eddie didn't see the Mexican anywhere. Maybe on the way back he'd stop into Willie's and ask if they knew anything about the Mexican having the truck—maybe Eddie could bring some new gossip to the diner tomorrow.

Across from Willie's, the convenience store used the historic corner door of the former bank building. When the welders were kids, this was the only bank in town. Now it glared with brightly lit beer ads and a scrolling lottery sign announcing the latest jackpot value.

EDDIE STOOD INSPECTING THE ROWS of canned drinks as cold air fell across his arms. His hesitation wasn't about which drink to choose, but rather if he should buy a lottery ticket. He didn't normally play the lottery, but with such a huge jackpot available, maybe he should just buy a ticket on the chance that if he won, he'd be able to ease his worries about his future and his legacy. He sighed and let go of the door handle and let the cooler thump itself closed.

As he turned away, Eddie felt a pain in his tricep—a firm grip squeezing his arm. A man's voice from behind was calm, "Don't move."

Eddie raised his palms in submission and said, "What do you want?"

"Don't ... move," the calm voice repeated.

The grip tightened and tugged Eddie closer to the drink cooler. As his feet shuffled, a loud screech of tires came from the street as a package delivery van collided with a building supply truck. Construction tools and crumbling sheetrock erupted onto the street. A three-foot length of steel rebar whizzed through the store window and impaled the self-serve lottery ticket machine, a mere four feet in front of Eddie. Sparks exploded and sizzled as the flashing panel was crushed.

Eddie fell to his knees as the man provided cover, holding

Eddie down until the sparking stopped. Eddie lowered his arms and looked up—it was the Mexican. Eddie stood and took a step back.

"See?" the Mexican said while adjusting his cowboy hat, "Don't move."

A small trickle of smoke rose out of the machine and the rebar protruded at the height of Eddie's chest. Had the Mexican not interfered, Eddie knew he would be dead.

"How did you—" Eddie stammered.

"We should talk, but not here."

THE MEXICAN LOWERED THE truck's tailgate and sat with his worn cowboy boots dangling from the ends of deep indigo blue jeans. He motioned for Eddie to do the same. Eddie leaned onto the side of the truck instead.

"It's almost as if you knew that would happen, and that I would be—" Eddie began.

"What's important is what *didn't* happen," the Mexican interrupted.

"But how?"

"Let's discuss this truck," the Mexican said as he tapped on the truck bed.

"We've been curious as to how you got it, me and the boys."

"I bought it from Mister Gorski, nothing fancy."

"But he was pretty healthy—his death was a surprise to everyone. How did you get him to sell it?"

"I offered him way more than it was worth," the Mexican said with a sly nod.

"He loved his truck. He wouldn't just—did you know ... he was going to die?"

The Mexican shrugged, "Maybe I just have good timing."

"What's so important about this truck?"

"I want you to have it. I want to give you the truck. I bought this truck so I could—actually, I want to trade with you. Trade for the truck."

"I don't have anything to trade."

"Come visit someone with me, just say 'hi'. That's it."

"That don't make sense—all I have to do to get this truck …
is visit someone?"

"Come with me, and say 'hi'. Then I'll propose what I'd like
to trade."

"I don't even know your name," Eddie said.

The Mexican extended his hand, "Alberto. The pleasure is all
mine. Confía en mí."

• • •

ALBERTO LET EDDIE DRIVE the truck for the full hour. Eddie
asked many questions about it and Alberto seemed to know
all the answers, even to questions about Old Man Gorski. They
arrived at half-past five, just as many small families were arriving.

"Grant Wood Elementary," Eddie read the sign aloud, "Fifth
Grade Science Fair."

Alberto smiled and said, "This is good."

THE TWO MEN WALKED INTO THE SCHOOL lunchroom and the
science fair was bustling. Alberto looked around and found a
table to his left positioned underneath a banner of multi-colored
handprints, the temporary legacy of all the students who attended the school.

"This way," Alberto said.

In front of the table stood a girl with long black hair, her skin
a smooth tawny. A handwritten name tag revealed her name to be
Meadow Feather Bravebird. She clasped her fingers at her waist,
nervously waiting for her next visitor.

Alberto and Eddie stepped up to the table. A tri-fold poster
board bore the title 'Genetics' and next to it was a candy model of
DNA made from licorice strands, gummy bears, and toothpicks.

"Can you tell me about your project?" Alberto asked.

The girl took a deep breath and turned to point at her poster board, "My project is about genetics and how genes pass on dominant and recessive traits. Some examples are dimples, freckles, and earlobes."

Alberto leaned toward the poster board and said, "Very interesting."

Eddie didn't know much about science, but he inspected the candy model and noticed one of the toothpicks had separated from the candy, threatening the whole thing with collapse.

"Looks like this red gummy bear doesn't want to cooperate," he said.

"Stupid thymine," the girl said as she squeezed the ends of the toothpicks to push the model back together, but the damaged bear wouldn't hold the toothpick.

"Can't you just replace it? It looks to be dried out," Eddie said, "Replace a bad red with a new red?"

The girl stopped adjusting the model and turned her eyes to Eddie.

"Back when I was a welder, we sometimes had to splice things together to fix them. Not too much different from this," he said.

Alberto smiled and placed his hand on Eddie's shoulder, "Thank you, Miss Bravebird, your project is outstanding."

The two men headed toward the exit and Alberto said to Eddie, "Very good."

As they walked, Eddie glanced back at the girl. She was still watching them.

Alberto added, "You seem to have made an impression on little Miss Bravebird."

THE CLOUDS GLOWED ORANGE as the men drove northwest along the river.

"So that's it?" Eddie asked Alberto.

"Yes sir."

They drove for a while without speaking, Alberto behind the wheel. The clouds were losing their orange shimmer and the sky was darkening and absorbing all shadows. Eddie thought about the school events he had attended when his own kids were small.

Alberto pointed to where the sun was dipping below the horizon, "What would you do if, one day, you knew it was going to be your last day alive? How would you spend that day?"

Eddie thought for a moment before saying, "I'd probably vacuum the whole house, to start."

"Vacuum?" Alberto said, surprised.

"Sure. I assume that the day *after* I die, people will be coming by the house. Don't want it looking junky and embarrass my wife."

Alberto smiled.

Eddie followed the headlights of a '79 Corvette headed in the opposite direction. He continued, "Maybe I'd go to the diner and thank the boys for being my friends. I'd tell Beth I always thought she had the most beautiful eyes I've ever seen. Probably things like that."

Alberto fixed his gaze ahead on the horizon, unblinking, "You're a good man. I suggest you do those things anyway."

Eddie looked at Alberto.

"How about you, what would you do?" Eddie asked.

Alberto let out a little sigh, "I don't ... really get to play that game."

EDDIE STEPPED OUT OF THE TRUCK and held on to the door frame. "Hey," he said as he turned back, "what happened back there, with that little Indian girl?"

"You mean Meadow Bravebird. I needed her to meet you—it was very important that she meet you."

Eddie shook his head, "I don't get it."

"Remember when I said I wanted to trade you for the truck?"

"Right. I still don't have anything, though. And I said 'hi' to the girl."

"This truck for the bar of gold that you brag about to your friends," Alberto said.

"My bar of gold? It's a fake, it's not worth twenty bucks."

"This truck for your fake bar of gold, what do you say?"

"My grandfather came home from Europe with that, said he bought it off a street vendor—the guy told him it was Hitler's gold. But I know it's a fake, covered in old paint or something. The story I tell the boys is more interesting, but not true."

"Deal then?"

• • •

AS THE WELDERS LEFT THE DINER the following Monday morning, they noticed Gorski's truck parked in Eddie's spot and Phil let out a grunt.

"Would you look at that, the Mexican's here," Richie said with snark.

Little Hank turned to the diner and said, "I didn't see him in there—did you see him?"

Phil stroked his beard as Eddie peered through the driver-side window.

"You guys wanna see something neat?" Eddie asked.

"Don't scratch it," Richie said.

Eddie looked around the parking lot with nervous eyes as he reached into his pocket and pulled out a key and opened the door. Eddie climbed in and started the engine.

"Sounds good, doesn't it?" he said with a smile.

"What the hell is going on, Eddie?" Richie scolded.

"It's mine. I bought it off the Mexican."

"How'd you do that?"

"I saw him by the old bank, asked if he wanted to sell, now it's mine."

"No way," Little Hank said as he slid his hand across the sidewall of the bed.

Phil became excited, "You gonna soup it up? Please tell me you're gonna soup it up."

"I don't know, it's pretty mint like it is," Eddie said, "I kinda like it plain."

"Like you," Richie said, "plain and boring."

• • •

IT WAS SPRINGTIME WHEN Alberto returned. As Eddie opened his front door, Alberto pointed to the truck in the driveway and complimented Eddie on his restraint for keeping it unmodified. Eddie said the raised white letter tires were the only thing he was brave enough to add.

The two men sat at the breakfast table and sipped a glass of fresh lemonade Beth had just prepared. Alberto reached into the breast pocket of his jacket and presented Eddie with an envelope.

"What's this?" Eddie asked.

"It's yours, open it."

Eddie lifted the flap and pulled out a cashier's check with his name on it.

"Eight hundred thousand dollars?" he said, confused.

"Yes."

"What's is for?"

"It's what's left over."

"From what?"

"There's a reason I needed your gold bar. Remember the little girl from the science fair? I sold your Hitler gold and set up a college trust fund for her—it's very important she goes to college. And, well, this is what's left over. I'm giving it back to you."

"Are you telling me that bar of gold was real?"

"I'm telling you your grandfather didn't get it from a street vendor. Let's leave it at that."

Eddie sat quietly, wondering if his grandfather had actually stolen it from Hitler's bunker. Had he been sitting on a fortune all these years?

"Why did you—why didn't you just keep it?"

"Remember our discussion coming back from that school? Well, it's time for me to vacuum my own house."

"You write the future, don't you?"

"You take the money. It's a much better payout than that lottery ticket that almost killed you," Alberto said as he stood and kissed Beth on the cheek.

Alberto gave Eddie a firm hug. Then Alberto slowly returned his worn cowboy hat to his head and showed himself to the door.

• • •

RICHIE, PHIL, AND EDDIE SAT on Little Hank's pastel floral-patterned couch. They had teased him about it for many years since retirement, but recently, things had been more somber.

"Little Hank, I think you've finally grown into your nickname with how much weight you've lost," Richie said.

Phil and Eddie laughed a little.

Little Hank lifted his hands from his recliner armrests and said, "I'll tell you what, though—I feel great. It's a bit scary being a test subject, but the cancer was gonna get me anyway—so figured I'd better try it out."

"Seriously," Eddie said, "you look great."

"What are they giving you?" Phil added.

"Nope, not medicine. It's something with genes, going right to the source."

"Amazing what they can do these days," Richie said.

"Guys, I've got something to say," Little Hank said as his tone became somber.

Silence fell across the room as the three shifted in their seats.

"We've been friends for a long time, all of us. And been retired for coming up on twenty years now. I'm not really supposed to say anything, but … this morning, they told me I've been cured."

Phil raised his eyebrows, "You're in remission? That's great!"

"No, not remission—I'm *cured*. Their treatments are showing permanent cures for all test subjects."

The men sat expressionless as they tried to absorb the news.

"A cure," Phil said, "for cancer? So nobody dies from cancer anymore?"

"Not all cancers, yet. But this one … gone," Little Hank exclaimed, "It won't be official until they publish the findings, but here I sit as living proof."

SOON THE MEN WERE ALL BACK together meeting at the diner every day. Little Hank was still a bit thin, but he said it was because of his superior fitness and claimed to be training for a marathon. This created handfuls of air to be swatted at him. The men had fewer condescending quips about the cars passing the corner at Thirteenth and Nichols, they seemed to have grown a bit more mature and content with themselves. They knew they almost lost Little Hank, and it scared them about their own mortality.

One morning in the diner, Little Hank pulled out a large manilla envelope with Eddie's name written on it. Little Hank told him it was included in some medical paperwork he received in the mail.

"What's in it?"

"I don't know. Somebody at the hospital wanted you to have it, I guess."

"Well? … Open it," Richie said.

Eddie lifted the flap and pulled out a '*Person of the Year*' issue of Time magazine. The photo was of a young woman in a white doctor's coat. The title banner read:

Meet Meadow Bravebird: The Destroyer of Cancer

Eddie froze. The other men sat on the edge of their seats as Eddie went pale.

A yellow sticky note tab protruded from the edge of the magazine. Eddie gripped the tab and opened the pages. He skimmed the article, landing on one particular paragraph:

> *When asked how she came up with the breakthrough procedure, Meadow points to a science fair from the fifth grade.*
>
> *"I did a presentation on genetic traits and had built a DNA model out of candy. It kept falling apart because one of the gummy bears was stale. A man walked up—and I remember him like it was yesterday, he said he was a welder—he suggested I swap out the bad gummy for a new one. And at that moment, like he was dictating my future, my pursuit of gene splicing was born."*

Eddie closed the magazine and grabbed his forehead. That little girl he spoke to for barely a moment was now leading the cure for cancer because of his words. He thought of Alberto. He thought of the rebar sticking out of the lottery machine. Eddie stood and scuttled toward the restroom, where he proceeded to vomit.

As Eddie hunched over the sink, he realized Alberto had orchestrated the whole chain of events to make that magazine end up in his hands while he sat with his cancer-free friend. Gene splicing, the truck, Old Man Gorski, Hitler's gold—it all connected to come together at this moment.

After a few minutes, Eddie returned to find the other men staring at him. Phil pointed to the magazine and said, "A welder? Who's the welder, Eddie?"

"Guys," Eddie said as he sat and raised his palms, "remember the Mexican? It was him, he—I don't know how to describe it."

Eddie paused and thought of the sunset and the '79 Corvette they had passed that evening. He thought of how Little Hank was forced to sell his yellow deuce coupe for the accumulating medical bills before he signed up for the experimental treatments.

"I—" Eddie stammered, "I—always wanted to thank you for being my friends." He looked around the table and nodded as he continued, "I'm glad we still got our health, and I'm thankful we stayed friends for basically our whole lives. I always wanted to say it, because I mean it. I do, I mean it."

Phil stroked his beard and nodded, "We've kinda had a good run, haven't we?"

"We have," Richie said.

Eddie stood and said, "Gentlemen, I need to go take care of something."

AS EDDIE DROVE PAST THE TWO artillery cannons at the old courthouse, he thought about the young sailors who fired them. He thought about his grandfather and the gold bar. He smiled at the idea of his grandfather standing in Hitler's bunker, smoking a victory cigar and sneaking a souvenir into his jacket.

The value of that gold bar to his grandfather wasn't that he could sell it and become rich, the value was that he could look at it for the rest of his life and know that he had won, that he and his war buddies had defeated evil and secured a better future for his children.

Eddie realized his own legacy didn't lie with anything he had accomplished himself, but that he had spliced his grandfather's victory onto little Meadow Bravebird, and ultimately to every future generation.

EDDIE ARRIVED HOME and found his wife sipping tea and reading a book at the kitchen table. He slowly pulled out a chair and sat.

"Beth, did I ever tell you that you have the most beautiful eyes I've ever seen?"

PROPER FAIRY

A FTER A LONG NIGHT THAT FOLLOWS a long day, the shortcut behind the pub—the footpath through my sparsely lit park—often seems like a good idea to a downtrodden man. But I don't mind; I've met many a great soul this way.

"I DON'T BELIEVE you," he said.

I assured him that I was most certainly a fairy.

"You're just a tiny little girl."

I hung in the nighttime air and let his thoughts settle. I had deliberately positioned myself between him and the lone streetlight, backlit fluttering wings are the best way to make a first impression, I've always thought.

"I don't think you're a fairy," his words slurred through whiskey fumes, "Maybe a moth. Are you a talking moth?"

I've never liked being called a moth, they're stupid and fly into lightbulbs and I don't look anything like a moth. I look like a fairy. But I understood his reluctance.

So I responded, "I will prove it to you."

He raised his wobbly arm and extended his finger, "Wait a minute little moth fairy, I heard a fairy tale once about ... fairies, and they say you will trick my mind to steal my soul. Maybe you're trying to trick my mind without me knowing. But I have a strong mind and I will not be tricked."

I responded, "I'm certain you have faith of strong mind and are not easily tricked, but I'm not here for tricks or to attempt any other nefarious deeds. I'm a simple, proper fairy."

He paused and took a deep breath. His eyes widened and blinked once before resuming their unfocused gaze. His feet, for the most part, maintained balance as he lowered his arm.

"What do you want from me little moth fairy?"

I crossed my arms and said, "First, please stop calling me a moth, they're stupid and fly into lightbulbs. I am a real fairy and respectfully request proper recognition."

His gruffness eased and he muttered, "Okay, fair enough."

I tapped him on the nose as I said, "Second, I must be real because I'm here in front of you, and you see me and are talking to me. So I, therefore, fulfill my responsibility of burden of proof for my claims of being real."

His jaw drooped, entranced by my words.

"Third," I continued, "fairies bring good luck, so bestowing good luck upon you would undoubtedly give you the remaining proof that I am actually a fairy."

He blinked as he said, "I could use some good luck."

"Fine, then we have a deal, I will bring you good luck and you will treat me like a proper fairy. I will visit you here again tomorrow."

I fluttered away and sat on a small tree branch to observe him. He looked up at the streetlight and watched the moths circling and colliding with the light. He squinted, uncertain if one of them was me.

· · ·

HE RETURNED THE NEXT EVENING looking for me. I had created the perfect balance of curiosity and doubt in his foggy brain to ensure he would return. He moved with hesitation, his focused eyes darting between bushes and tiny tree branches.

A few times he even looked up at the streetlight to see if any of the moths were me. They, of course, were not.

After a few minutes of watching him, watching his caution turn into frustration, I fluttered over his head and resumed my backlit position.

"There you are, little fairy! I wasn't sure if I had imagined you," his voice dripping in relief.

"I told you I would return, and I always keep my word."

He wasn't sure what to say, or what he was supposed to do next. I waited for him to decide.

"I had some good fortune today. One of my most stubborn accounts opened their purse and poured a bunch of money into my business. I couldn't help but wonder if that was because of you."

"It was," I said with the slightest demure smile, "I'm glad you like my work."

"This is incredible. You bring me good luck and all I have to do is ... is ... I'm sorry, I've forgotten what it is I have to do."

"Our deal was that I bring you good luck, and you treat me like a proper fairy. Very simple," I said matter-of-factly.

"Yeah, yeah that's right. Just, treat you like a fairy," he brimmed with relief, "This is great."

"I will resume tomorrow, and meet you here again in the evening. I anticipate good feedback."

"Yes," he said, "that sounds great! I will be here."

I batted my eyelashes then fluttered away to sit on my favorite tree branch and observe. He scratched his ear and smiled as he scurried away, too excited to look up at the streetlight.

• • •

AS EXPECTED, HE RETURNED the next evening, this time more patient in his search for me. I didn't feel like making him wait since I was getting hungry, so I flittered past his face and resumed my backlit allure. For the second night in a row, he didn't smell like alcohol.

"Fairy, fairy, what a great day! Thank you, thank you!"

With the slightest twinkle in my eye, I said, "You're welcome."

He spun around, so filled with joy, and tapped his feet twice.

"This is great, this is amazing!"

I approached him with a coquettish smile, "So would you agree that I am actually a fairy?"

He gushed, "Yes, yes, you are very much a fairy! A wonderful, proper fairy!"

"So would you agree that I am fully entitled to do my proper fairy things?"

"Oh, yes—"

But before he could say anything more, I grabbed his lips, opened my mouth much wider than it would seem I should be able to, and took a deep inhale. His arms went limp and fell to his sides, his eyes glazed over as his pupils dilated.

As I hovered away from his mouth, he attempted to speak, slow with slurred consonants, "Whah are you dooeen?"

I held onto the breath, enjoying the surge of life. It had been a while since I had eaten, and I was starving. I clenched my fists and felt the rush of energy. He never moved, his gaze fixed on me.

As a proper fairy, I gave him a proper answer, "I, sir, am collecting on your side of the deal. I brought you good luck and now you are letting me do my proper fairy things. Which at this point, is to consume your soul. I thank you for adhering to our deal."

I gave him a moment for my words to seep into understanding. Then I grabbed his lips again and took an even deeper inhale of his soul. This second one seals the deal.

His body withered and I clenched him by the throat to allow his clothes to fall to the ground. He was now slightly smaller than me, but with those buggy eyes and powdery skin, he should never be mistaken for a fairy. Moths don't look anything like fairies.

I let go of his throat and he flapped his wings as he headed toward the streetlight. I waited long enough to watch him collide once with the lightbulb.

To be honest, that is my favorite part.

BURNT EDGES

THE WIND BLEW OUT OF THE northeast this morning, carrying with it the sickly sweet smell of burnt oats. I peered through my front window to the smokestacks of the oat factory; sharp, immutable edges on the horizon standing firm beyond the swaying branches of my neighborhood trees. The low, ominous clouds were painted along the bottom edge in wisps of red, tinted by the glow of the factory's giant electric sign. They seemed to smolder from the inside, churning, but not quite igniting.

I was on my way to Iowa City to visit a friend, so I woke early to ensure I arrived before the rains hit. I kissed my wife as she slept, and after stepping outside, I became lost in time when the full strength of the malodorous winds hit me. I leaned against the front porch pillar and crossed my arms. It brought me back to middle school.

I REMEMBER THE FIRST DAY of sixth grade and the terror I held behind that half-smile. The morning had been chaotic at home. Not only was I starting middle school, but my little sister was starting kindergarten. Since my stepdad had taken over the house,

I had learned to mask fear, to mask most emotions. My sister, also scared to death of a new school, had a meltdown that morning and my role became to step aside, remain quiet, and fight the urge to vomit.

My mom made it clear she wouldn't be packing me a sack lunch anymore since my sister needed the extra attention in the mornings. And it was the first time I walked to school by myself. Mom used to walk me to the elementary school and push my sister in the stroller, but now my stepdad insisted on taking them both to my sister's drop-off. He said that boys should be tough and shouldn't need anyone to take them to school. So I walked alone.

I had no idea how the hot lunch line worked so I hung against the wall until I saw how the other kids did it. There were two entree choices that day: rectangular pizza slices from a giant pan or gravy-covered meat stuff. The lunchroom filled with the sickly sweet burnt smell of that assembly-line pizza.

The woman serving the hot meals was large and intimidating with dark eyes and a strong jawline. The lunchroom uniforms were crimson-colored, long-sleeved oxford shirts, and the woman's stocky build was barely contained within. I lifted a tray and slid it up in front of the pizza. The woman's nametag was a black embossed oval that read 'Miss Haskell'. She was maybe the same age as my mother, it was hard to tell because she wore a hair net and her hair was pulled back into a bun that reminded me of my grandmother.

"Pizza—Salisbury steak," she said in a raspy smoker's voice.

"Pizza please," I said as I pointed to the tray of overcooked pizza.

She lifted a rectangular corner piece and dropped it onto a foam plate, which she slid across the counter.

I reached out but stopped before touching the plate. The edges of the pizza were burnt on two sides with a crispy trim of blackened cheese.

"Could I have a middle piece instead?" I asked shyly.

Miss Haskell tilted her head and placed her fists on her hips.

"You'll get what I give you," she barked, "now move along."

I lowered my head in embarrassment and pulled the plate onto my tray. I could feel her piercing glare on the back of my neck as I moved forward in the line.

Kids from several elementary schools combined into middle school and the friendships from the last several years seemed to have been erased. I sat by myself for lunch that day.

I kept my eyes down, but about halfway through eating I noticed Miss Haskell having a discussion with the principal. I'm pretty sure they were talking about me. I was certain I was in trouble for talking back about the pizza and I started to think of ways to deny it to my stepdad. The principal nodded and headed directly toward me. My back began to sweat and a rush of heat filled my head.

The principal was a rotund man with a monk-shaped bald spot and a thick brown mustache. He reminded me of a Saturday morning cartoon character. He circled the table and stood behind me. Very slowly, he leaned forward and smiled to get my attention. When I saw him out of the corner of my eye, I was startled by his enormous smile.

"Hello," he said, "I'm Mr. Schaeffer, the principal."

I could only think of the ways I was going to deny being inconsiderate to Miss Haskell.

"I try to meet all the students at least once, so I thought I'd stop by."

I envisioned the punishment I would face when I got home.

"Hi," I said as I dropped my eyes to the table.

"I was over there talking to Miss Haskell—you've met her, right? I wanted to let you know that if you have any problems, any problems whatsoever, all you have to do is speak up and someone will help."

He waved his hand across the lunchroom monitors standing on the perimeter of the room and said, "We're all here to help. How does that sound to you?"

I dropped my eyes to the table again and said, "Fine."

"Well, good!" he said with a big smile.

Mr. Schaeffer stood upright and placed his hand on the base of my neck, I winced from the discomfort. He squeezed a little harder and I pulled away from the increasing pain. I looked up to find Miss Haskell standing with her arms crossed and her face wearing a blank expression.

"I'm sorry, did I hurt you?" the principal asked.

"No—no, I'm fine."

"Well, okay then," he said as he left.

• • •

THE SECOND ENTREE OPTION changed every day, but pizza was guaranteed and inevitably filled the air with that sickly sweet burnt smell. Miss Haskell barked out the choices. I chose the pizza. She dropped a piece on a plate and slide it across the countertop.

After a few weeks, the other boys became bolder and teased me quite a bit. I also heard them say mean things about Miss Haskell. They said she was in a biker gang and that one of their cousins saw Miss Haskell riding a big motorcycle and was covered in tattoos of fairies and demons. They said she had once murdered someone and was still on parole. They said she called herself 'Haskell' because it sounded like 'has-killed', which they were convinced she had. They said the reason the lunch ladies wore blood-colored shirts was to hide the evidence of the kids they kill to make the pizza sauce.

Miss Haskell was consistently gruff. It didn't matter who you were or what you ordered, your food got dropped onto a foam plate and forcefully slid across the countertop. As the year moved on, the other kids became more disrespectful to everyone, especially Miss Haskell. I kept away from them as much as I could since they found it funny to intentionally bump into me.

MY LITTLE SISTER WAS DOING amazing in kindergarten, according to my stepdad. I've always received the highest praise from my art teachers and Mom used to proudly display my work on the refrigerator door. But that year, it had all been replaced by my sister's smears of primary colors on construction paper and cotton balls glued to popsicle sticks. I stopped bringing my projects home even though I was winning blue ribbons in interschool competitions.

On Sunday mornings, we went to church. My stepdad made us arrive early to ensure we sat in the front center pew. While we sat and waited, if my sister fidgeted, he tickled her. But if I became uncomfortable and wiggled even the smallest amount, he grabbed my thigh with his steel-claw grip and whispered a painful threat from his unmoving smile. He waited until about fifteen minutes before mass started, then he got up and left. He'd say he was going out for a quick smoke, but I knew his ego loved having all eyes in the parish on him as he walked to the back of the church. I breathed easier when he wasn't around.

IN THE LUNCHROOM, IT WAS common for Miss Haskell to stare at me with crossed arms while I sat by myself. One day Mr. Schaeffer came into the lunchroom and talked to Miss Haskell. Miss Douglas, the woman who gave us our milk cartons, joined them. I noticed Miss Haskell kept tapping her pointed finger firmly into her palm. Something serious was happening. Mr. Schaeffer casually walked around the lunchroom, smiling at students and asking how their days were going.

He circled me and placed his hand on my shoulder. I winced.

"Hello, big man," he said ironically since I was one of the smallest boys in the school.

"How's everything been going in the sixth grade?" he continued.

"Fine."

"Good ... good," he said as he squeezed my shoulder on each word.

The pain was intense, he was squeezing right on my biggest bruise. I tried to pull away, but his grip was firm. I looked up to see Miss Haskell standing with her arms crossed.

"I'm sorry, did I hurt you again?" he asked.

"I'm fine, I just ... fell off my bike on Saturday."

"Well, that can certainly happen, believe you me!" he said with a laugh, "Especially since it rained all weekend—it's very easy to lose control in such a downpour."

"It is. I did."

Later that day, the P.E. teacher sent me to the office after I changed out of my uniform. He told me the secretary was missing a permission slip or something. But when I got there, Mr. Schaeffer and Miss Haskell were waiting, and they took me into the nurse's office.

IT WAS A PAINFUL AND NORMAL week at home. On Sunday we went to church. I wasn't allowed breakfast that morning for some angry reason, so when my stepdad left for his smoke, I begged my mom to let me go to the lobby and get a drink of water. She agreed and told me to hurry back.

I took a big long drink and as I wiped my lips on my sleeve, I looked out the lobby's side window and spotted my stepdad outside behind our car. But instead of having a smoke, he was surrounded by three large bikers covered in leather and chains—their big Harleys parked just a few feet away.

When I saw my stepdad's frightened eyes, I noticed the shortest of the bikers was Miss Haskell, and her finger was pointed right at his throat. She leaned into him and tapped against his chest very slowly. Their faces were probably only six inches apart.

I knew I would be in huge trouble if my stepdad saw me, so I walked as fast as I could back to the front pew. Mass started on time and he wasn't back yet. My leg started to bounce as adrenaline raced through my body. Mom put her hand on my knee and told me to sit still. It took all of my energy to keep that leg from moving.

When my stepdad came back, he wore an expression I'd never seen on him; he was terrified. We did all the church things of standing and singing, but oddly, he never looked at me once. I didn't know what to expect when we would arrive home that morning, but he never touched me again.

The next day in the lunch line, Miss Haskell barked the entrees, I answered, and the plate slid across the countertop. I placed it on my tray, but before I turned to leave, I did something I had never done—I looked up at Miss Haskell. She held an emotionless gaze for a few seconds, then said, "Move along!" and waved her hand toward Miss Douglas. For the first time that year, I smiled at school.

• • •

I UNCROSSED MY ARMS AND STEPPED off the front porch. The ominous clouds, seemingly burnt along the lower edge, were churning stronger and I had had enough of that oat factory smell.

I made it to the university before the rain and parked near the hospital entrance. They directed me to the proper floor and room and I set a small vase of flowers next to Miss Haskell's bed.

We chatted and laughed for a while and she asked about my niece and nephew. I asked her if she knew what the kids called her in school.

"I have no idea. But those red shirts sure came in handy," she said with a wink.

"How long can you stay?" she asked.

"I figure I'll stay a while, push you around in the chair—get some wheels back underneath you again."

Miss Haskell gave me a modest smile.

"Thank you," she said.

"For what?"

"For being strong … and surviving."

"Well, I had a guardian angel, you know," I said as I squeezed her hand.

I nodded as I thought back to the first day of middle school and said, "There's something I noticed, something you didn't think I noticed."

Miss Haskell raised her eyebrows.

"That very first piece of pizza was the only burnt edge you ever gave me," I said, "Every other one was always from the center. That wasn't quite random, was it?"

Miss Haskell shrugged and said, "Some people deserve better than the burnt edges."

BLACKOUT DAY

EVERYONE WILL WANT TO KILL you, she told me. I assured her I was but an unbiased traveler.

A small village like this has always been self-sustaining, suspicious of outsiders. She embraced me into her home and we became family. She had been alone a long time, the lone wolf of the village. But then it was the two of us. She spoke of the tradition that was Blackout Day, where the other homesteads of the village drew blinds tight and stayed inside with loved ones.

Nearing dusk, their fires were kindled. With much laughter and hugging, the old games of the ancestors were played by all. It was a celebration of the Moon, and of life. Once the doors were locked, they remained locked until daybreak.

Blackout Days were not to be ignored. Blackout Days were sacred, valued by all, once per month. Roughly.

The next morning, the villagers greeted each other over coffee and wished each other a good day. When asked how the night went, the answer was always the same, *It was wonderful, the Moon has granted us life!*

Dispersing, they left bootprints in the snow, off to embrace the new day.

• • •

SOME WILL WANT TO KILL you, we told him. He noted he was but a transient wayfarer.

We embraced him into our home as a new family member. Our numbers had grown, as some of the villagers couldn't help but join us. We described to him the sacred tradition that was Blackout Day. We spoke of the ancestors, and the traditional fires, and the playing of games. We spoke of the Moon, and of life, and of locked doors.

The morning villagers still greeted each other over coffee and wished each other a good day. They still answered the same, *It was wonderful, the Moon has granted us life!*

We tried to mimic their rested demeanor, mimic their response, *The Moon has granted us life*. But we had become skeptical of such things.

• • •

NOBODY TRIES TO KILL us anymore. We are all family, and the villagers are us.

Outsiders passing through are rare, but they will be welcomed into the family too, just like the rest of us were. We still have blackout days, once per month. Roughly.

Doors are not locked any more, the old games of the ancestors are not played, and fires burn out untended. The blackout days are still sacred, dreaded by all.

In the morning we greet each other over coffee and wish each other a good day. We never ask how the night went, we already know—we celebrated the Moon, we growled, we howled, we left paw prints in the snow.

And we all blacked out.

ENCORE

EDITH SALISBURY PREENED into the coffee shop with her nose held high and her pinky finger outstretched from behind a flowery silk shawl. She looked down upon a young couple whose attention was buried in their mobile phones, watching self-aggrandizing video clips of unknown strangers dancing in public and performing juvenile stunts. Edith knew these two kids could not possibly recognize her—they probably hadn't seen any films released more than fifteen years ago. But their parents, had they been present, might possibly have had an inkling of who Edith was, but only if they themselves were connoisseurs of classic golden-era films.

Edith ordered a simple black coffee. The barista vaguely remembered Edith from having served her many times before, but he didn't know her name or anything personal about her. She was just another flamboyant old woman in a city of endless attention-seeking characters.

It was normal for customers to order drinks with multiple fancy adjectives of flavorful decoration. Specifying excessive options assured their name be written on the cup. It was an ego-centric validation provided by the coffee shop to their pretentious customers. Having only ever ordered a plain black coffee with no fancy adjectives or decorative flavors, Edith remained nameless to anyone handing her a drink.

But Edith entered the shop with a new attitude this time. Her step had a bounce and she wore an expression of satisfaction about the event she had scheduled later in the day. So she asked for her name to be written on the cup. The young barista with a pierced nose and woven dreadlocks hesitated as he placed Edith's simple drink in front of her on the countertop. She crossed her arms and insisted her name be written in full. Even with the drink easily within reach, she repeated her name to him and spelled it out to avoid confusion. Edith knew anyone who served her today would hold bragging rights tomorrow. She was doing him a favor.

MUCH EARLIER IN LIFE, it was unnecessary for Edith to ever spell her name for anyone. She could walk into a restaurant in New York City on a bustling Saturday night and immediately be escorted to a private table. She could arrive at a sold-out play in London and be seated next to the director within minutes. She could enter the Opéra Garnier in Paris just before showtime and be fanning herself in box seats just as the curtain rose. Everyone knew Edith Salisbury, she was the most famous and adored actress in the world.

At the height of her fame, Edith met Ty Richardson in Los Angeles one month before her twenty-fifth birthday. They both had been invited to the governor's annual black-tie gala where every notable celebrity and self-important politician mingled. Ty was an actor too; in New York City he was the up-and-coming star of Broadway. His coal-black hair was always tidy, except for one strategically loose tuft falling across his forehead. His build was solid and his pragmatic demeanor was shaped by his upbringing in a working-class New Jersey family. Ty was a man with grit who could get into an afternoon street fight, toss down a whiskey or three with the boys, and still command a standing ovation on stage in the evening.

Ty was aware of Edith and her world-class notoriety but had never seen one of her films, the kind he referred to as 'love stories for dames'. When Ty and his friends sat in a motion picture theater, the screen filled with action—bank robberies, wild west gunfights, or mobsters unleashing Tommy guns.

The governor introduced Ty to Edith at the beginning of the evening just as cocktails arrived on silver carts. Ty kissed the back of Edith's hand and the governor giggled with excitement as Edith responded with her famous million-dollar smile. A simple wave of the governor's hand to strike up the band relieved the party of its stuffy formalities and the dance floor filled. Ty and Edith floated across the room with complementary footwork and glossy eyes for each other. The other guests were not oblivious to their chemistry and scuttlebutt traveled across tables, leaked through the lobby, and onto the front page of the morning paper. The most beautiful star in film and the biggest heartthrob on Broadway fell in love that night.

EDITH HEADED EAST TO be with Ty and they were soon living in New York City in a posh high-rise on the Upper East Side. Edith was used to a high-profile life in California, but in New York, she felt like a princess on top of the world. News photographers spent so much time trying to capture them that they were dubbed the Central Park Fireflies due to the flickering of their camera flashes in the nighttime. At one point, Edith's agent hired sets of look-alike models to provide a diversion just so Edith and Ty could simply leave their building for a night out. The world went wild for their fame and blossoming romance.

The contrast of Edith's pure and pleasant disposition to Ty's rough-and-tumble street gruff earned them the collective nickname 'Sugar & Salt'. Life magazine reportedly offered the couple a preposterous amount of money to publicly discuss their unlikely relationship in an exclusive article, but the offers went unanswered. Speculation swirled into a larger storm.

The eyes on Hollywood went wild when on a Thursday in September, the Los Angeles airport crawled with a significantly high number of celebrities flying to New York City. When questioned about their trip, every single one claimed to be going shopping for the holidays.

That Saturday morning, 5th avenue was closed to traffic in front of St. Patrick's Cathedral, and sidewalks were barricaded to contain onlookers. Four majestic white horses pulling a flower-covered carriage waited for the newlyweds to emerge and lead a procession worthy of European royalty.

The ride to the Waldorf Astoria was merely a few blocks but the spectacle was worthy of a parade in itself. Fans lined the streets and waved and screamed as the couple passed. Several young girls were brought to tears when Edith smiled at them. One girl who was lucky enough to catch a blown kiss from Ty lost her breath and fainted. Camera bulbs flashed and the world was introduced to a new aristocracy.

CRACKS STARTED TO SHOW almost immediately while honeymooning in Italy. Ty became annoyed with the attention and the size of the crowd gathering outside their private villa. He had been pacing and drinking all day when he left the property and punched a photographer on the street. Photos of the ruckus surfaced and were soon plastered on the front of every newspaper from Rome to Los Angeles.

Many people heard a loud commotion from inside their villa, with Ty yelling at Edith and breaking dishes. On their return flight to New York, other passengers noticed that Edith never spoke to Ty and hid her face when anyone passed through the aisle.

Back home, a new Broadway show was considering Ty as the leading man when he was arrested at a seedy bar in Brooklyn. He and his old neighborhood buddies were celebrating the birthday of his best friend when a group of shore-leave sailors teased Ty that he must be a soft pansy to enjoy acting in plays and crying like a woman. Ty broke the jaw of one of the sailors and ended up in jail. He later found out it was the mayor's son he had incapacitated, and the newspapers went wild.

EDITH'S MOTHER REPEATEDLY BEGGED her to take an overdue rest. Edith found solace in her mother's words and agreed she needed a break from the negative attention of Ty's behavior and increasing burden. Edith came from humble beginnings and at her mother's pleading, Edith spent three weeks visiting her childhood home back in Hannibal, Missouri.

Every day after breakfast, she read her Bible on the porch swing and took a leisurely walk. Some days she went down the hill to watch the freight barges pass. Those boats lived a lonely existence, she thought, traversing the length of the mighty river while never gleaning attention from anyone on shore. On other days she walked up to Lover's Leap and thought about the legend that gave the rock formation its name. She found it difficult to imagine the mindset of someone who could be in such a hopeless mental state as to make that deathly leap.

Regardless of what occupied her mornings, every afternoon she visited the Thatcher theater and helped tutor the after-school acting classes. It gave her comfort working with kids in the same theater where she had found her love of acting. She laughed with them. They became silly together. They all clomped around the stage like monsters and roared.

Edith talked about Hollywood and told funny stories about her friends, who also happened to be the big screen's most famous faces. She emphasized how as actors, the kids should always take every role seriously—it didn't matter if the show was on a massive soundstage in Burbank or a tiny theater stage in Hannibal. But most importantly, she taught them that fully committing to the role was the most important thing they could do.

Edith's visit to Hannibal was a therapeutic and joyful time for her. She relaxed and reconnected with family as well as the modest townspeople with whom she grew up. But underneath it all, the lure of Hollywood crept back in and she missed the high-wattage attention. In Hannibal, she had no chauffeur. She waited in lines. She washed her own clothes. In Hannibal, she was unimportant.

Ty phoned for Edith many times but her mother wouldn't allow Edith to speak with him until she was showing significant signs of emotional healing. When Ty was finally able to get through to Edith, he apologized profusely and promised he was becoming a better man. He promised he had stopped drinking and carousing with his childish buddies. Edith decided to return to Los Angeles to take a few business meetings before meeting Ty in New York to mend their relationship.

THE ABRUZZO ITALIAN RESTAURANT in Santa Monica was the birthplace of many of the biggest Hollywood films. Lawrence of Arabia secured financing there. Casablanca's cast was chosen by studio executives there. And Edith Salisbury had been pitched starring roles in two dozen films there. Whenever the telephone rang in advance of Edith's arrival, the private dining suite on the second floor was prepared with candles and a vase of fresh roses before she arrived.

Upon Edith's return to Abruzzo, her agent did not mince words: Ty's increasingly bad reputation was damaging both of their careers. Edith argued that she was at the top of her acting game and the studios would be foolish not to feature her in a big-budget drama. Her agent made it clear that the studios had no interest in greenlighting a film with Edith when Ty's reckless behavior could jeopardize its opening day audience draw. Ty's downward spiral was a liability to the studio, and Edith's star power fell along with him.

Their divorce was initiated when Confidential Magazine

broke the news of Ty's numerous infidelities across New York City. Newspaper headlines roared in bold type announcing:

'The Spicy Lives of Sugar & Salt'

A circus of invasive journalists overwhelmed Edith, who, from the embarrassment of it all, never returned to New York.

On the day their marriage was officially dissolved, typesetters had already prepared the morning paper:

'Sugar & Salt: Careers Cooked'

Ty's drinking and bar fights continued out of control and rumors roared when he was photographed with a mob boss's wife. One cold and rainy Sunday morning in Hell's Kitchen, Ty Richardson was found dead in a back alley with a bullet in his head.

EDITH NEVER STARRED IN A FILM again. Ten years after the divorce, the best she could do was land a few small roles on low-rated network TV shows. Ten years after that, nobody cared who Edith was anymore. She had been the world's most beloved candle, but now her flame was extinguished.

Some rumors claimed Edith had returned to Hannibal to teach acting classes to children. Other rumors had her homeless in West Hollywood. Nobody was certain exactly what happened to Edith over the years, but if you paid close attention, you could spot a flamboyant old woman ordering a simple black coffee at an unassuming coffee shop.

THE BARISTA WITH THE PIERCED nose and woven dreadlocks raised his eyebrows as he said, "Are you serious?"

Edith instructed him to write her full name on the cup. She spelled it again.

He sighed as he reached for the black marker. With every letter, he paused and looked at Edith in defiance. After he finished her name, he drew a princess crown and slowly turned the cup to show her.

"Is that okay, lady?" he said with an edge of sarcasm, "It's my best penmanship."

Edith looked down her nose and said, "Very good. Now, remember it."

EDITH ENTERED THE LOBBY of the Uptown Grand Plaza hotel and asked to be escorted to the Sky Lounge. She was informed it was closed in preparation for a private party later that evening. Edith scoffed and revealed that the party was in fact for her, the legendary Ms. Edith Salisbury. She described how it was to be a highly publicized event where she would launch her big encore, where her fame would be revived in bold type on the front of tomorrow's newspaper.

The Sky Lounge was locked when the concierge arrived with Edith. A simple turn of the key opened into the warm city air with blue skies framed by large open windows under the roofline. Edith smirked and insisted that she be left alone to prepare for her performance without distraction.

She paced slowly around the unattended rooftop lounge, her feet shuffling on patterned carpet that waited to be converted into wedding receptions, conference parties, and in her case, a newsworthy encore. Her hands moved gracefully as she waved toward where her leading man would certainly be standing. He will be young and strong, with masculine features, bearing an uninterested gaze. Her memories of Ty were mostly of his broken years, but if she were to conjure up the original Ty—the one with the coal-black hair and pragmatic demeanor—her leading man would stand before her with that same handsome, charming grit.

Edith moved out onto the sunlit deck and formed a rectangle with her fingers, "Camera right here, the hills will make a wonderful backdrop. Why, yes, this will do just fine."

She waved her hands around dismissively, "Too many people, step away from Ms. Salisbury, please."

Turning to the imaginary cameraman, she said, "We can't

have so many people in the shot, don't forget who's the focus here."

Edith moved to the edge of the building and pressed her shoulder into the decorative stone ledge crowning the wall. "No, no, this won't do at all. Much too high."

She touched a finger against her lips and scanned the edges of the party room and spotted a folding chair. Her encore was not going to be ruined by the lack of a simple prop chair.

After she straightened the chair and tested its sturdiness, she stepped up to diminish the height of the wall. "That's *much* better," she said.

She twisted her hips and sat on the sunny ledge. "Wonderful," she said as she crossed her legs and cupped her hands across her knee. Edith remembered holding a similar pose beneath the Chabaud Mozart at the Palais Garnier for the cover of a Paris fashion magazine fifty or sixty years earlier. She remembered all the times blinding camera flashes constricted her pupils, leaving her beautiful blue eyes glowing for her admirers. She remembered the young girls who cried when she approached the ropes of a red carpet to shake their hands. Edith remembered it all as she lifted her hand and waved like the Queen of England—who, consequently, had taught Edith the technique personally.

Edith knew an encore was her last chance to regain the spotlight and be famous once more. But she also knew the reality that she would never again enjoy the stardom she longed for. So she straightened her legs and swung them over the edge. With a little push, she was weightless.

Had it been the era when young boys wearing newsboy caps hawked newspapers on the street corner, Edith's encore would have been the headline in bold type she hoped for. But there were no more paperboys and no wooden newsstands on street corners. And since the tragic news of Edith's encore was buried deep behind a few phone screen swipes and taps, her encore went unnoticed.

THE YOUNG COUPLE WAS IN the coffee shop again the next day, with noses against their mobile phones, watching the latest posts of sophomoric absurdity. A young woman wearing a backpack covered in patches of cartoon characters entered and waved to the barista with the pierced nose and dreadlocks.

He could barely hold back his excitement as he clapped his hands and told her, "Did you hear who was in here yesterday? Oh my god!"

The girl's eyes lit up, "I heard there was a commotion, what happened—who was it?"

"That viral video guy with drinking straws in his earlobes—you know, *Dolla-Dash The Hype*. He came in just after my shift, I can't believe I missed him!"

"He was in here? Right here? Oh my god, such a famous person stood right where I'm standing! This is so exciting—I have to post this to my followers, they are not going to believe it. I'm going to get so many likes on this!"

GLOVES

WHEN I UNFOCUS MY EYES just the right amount, the lights flicker and dance and smear in the most beautiful and random way. I prefer to watch them pass from left to right. Left to right, like time. I know this representation of time is purely arbitrary, but, for me, time moves left to right.

Sometimes I can't get a seat on this side of the train, facing the left-to-right window show, so I'll stand to ensure my view. Once in a while, someone will motion for me to take an open seat on the opposite side, but I'd be facing the wrong way and it would seem weird and unnatural to see time flowing backward. So I flex a simple smile and hold up a friendly palm.

Of course, my palm is always encased within a black dress glove. Hardy enough to fend off the chilliest of days, but not the type you'd wear during a mushy snowball fight. I must always treat my hands with respect, and cold wet gloves during winter are rather disrespectful.

But these gloves are perfect for me; I can touch the things I need, yet never touch anyone else. I'm an asymptomatic transmitter. With a simple touch from my bare skin, I will pass the virus.

It's a virus, I think. It behaves like a virus, making itself at home, then at its own pace, revealing its symptoms. I don't know what this virus is called, or where I got it, but I definitely transmit it. For a long time, I didn't know I was the cause of the infections, but over the years I figured out the pattern. I'm asymptomatic so I don't feel the effects, but everyone I've infected has. And as far as I've seen, I'm the only transmitter on Earth.

Sometimes as I watch the lights go racing by, left to right, I think of one particular infection I caused. It sits high in my thoughts mostly because of the magnitude of the ripples which still vibrate to this day. But also, because of the gentle, positive soul of the young man, and what he longed to be.

And what I did to him.

I FOUND MYSELF IN A TINY COFFEE SHOP, one block north of the baseball stadium and next to a shuttered souvenir stand. It was a new coffee shop at the time, it hadn't yet become famous as the launching point of such a major musical star. I discovered it that night only because I had been out wandering the neighborhoods, enjoying the holiday decorations in the crisp December air. And my fingers had become cold.

The young man perched atop a stool, playing his acoustic guitar and singing into a dented microphone. The coffee shop wasn't really big enough to need amplified sound, but I guess it helped us to hear over the harsh chaos of the coffee grinders. I remember thinking his pitch was occasionally flat. And I also wondered if perhaps he wasn't wearing that bright red sweater, he might be more comfortable.

But I think that was the point. He didn't want to be comfortable, he wanted to suffer.

I listened to his strings resonate and his fingertips squeak. I listened to his lyrics. For me, he wasn't the background noise of someone droning through their anemic setlist, he was confident in his playing and he was confident in his message. He had things to say to the world, he had a world to change.

But then he would speak between songs. This was an insecure kid who probably drove down from a north-shore mansion, and he probably got that sweater as a gift from his mother. His songs told me he would never pick out that sweater for himself, but he wore it to suffer. He wore it to sweat. He wore it to feel the weight of a facade that in no way represented the soulful wings folded tightly on his back, waiting to spread, waiting to soar, and waiting to change the world.

But I've been around long enough to recognize that those wings would never open if he stayed living in that lakeshore mansion. They would never open if the only suffering he would experience was wearing that bright red, sweat-inducing, embarrassing gift from his mother. And it made me uneasy. This young man was destined to soar.

I sipped another coffee or two and enjoyed his performance. I stayed until the end. My whole visit brimmed with uncertainty and indecision; I have a general rule to remain unbiased and let fate play out how it may. But this situation, for this young man, at this time, seemed somehow different to me.

I approached him and shook his hand. I complimented him on his message and his lyrical depth. I made him promise that this was only the beginning. I made him promise that this would be his last performance in that red sweater. He giggled and thanked me. Where no one else had even acknowledged his playing, some unknown one-gloved man had just infected his future.

I never went to that coffee shop again, it wasn't my neighborhood and I had since moved on to wandering other areas and other cities.

I THOUGHT OF THE YOUNG MAN over the next months, and over the next years you couldn't avoid him. His doleful songs topped the radio and his face was on many concert t-shirts. Every once in a while he would stop back at that famous coffee shop, unannounced, and perform an impromptu set. Within minutes the streets would be flooded with fans trying to get a glimpse of him performing on the same stool where he started.

But that was only half of it, for I had given him the virus. His wings would have never opened without it, so for that, I feel good. But knowing that I covered him in the blanket of the virus, I struggle with that part. I don't know what the virus is really called, or where I got it, but I've since given it a name: *Suffering*. The young man rose quickly because of the virus, but he fell just as fast. The virus is a worthy adversary.

Now people visit his tombstone and leave bottles of whiskey. They sit with him and smoke a cigarette and cry. His words touched them at their core. They mourn their future without his heart and his wisdom, they mourn for his guidance.

TODAY I'M STANDING, AGAIN with unfocused eyes. I'm watching the lights flicker and dance and smear in a beautiful and random way—left to right. I hold on tightly with my new gloves.

An elderly woman had entered the train earlier and I offered her my seat. She accepted, so now I stand next to her. After a while, she compliments me on my coat and gloves and mentions that her husband's fingers get cold easily in this weather, and how hard it is to find good gloves. She compliments me again and says that my beautiful gloves are probably a lifesaver at this time of year.

I smile and place a covered hand on top of hers.

"Yes, ma'am. Yes they are."

FOR THE PRICE OF PANCAKES

———————

I STOOD IN A CHURCH'S BELL TOWER, looking down over a crowded piazza. The faithful bustled below with determination to arrive to mass on time. Families, walking side by side, moved in waves with a constant flow until they reached the holy steps and found turbulence in their feet. Compressed and slowing, the waves of people shifted and grabbed handrails and bumped each other as they crept up the stairs, then dissipated like a mist through the open doors.

A man dressed in black rose from the tumbling water of the piazza fountain. He emerged, somehow, with completely dry clothes. A black cape billowed behind him and his face hid beneath a black Cordovan hat. He slowly tipped his head to reveal mask-covered eyes, dark empty windows that were now locked with mine.

The man in black lifted his hand and thrust a pointed finger at me, causing the bell in the church tower to roar with a deafening gong. The deep reverberating tone transformed into a sharp high-pitched bell that pierced the darkness beyond my eyelids. As the ringing entered my ears, a heavy wave of pain thrust inward to split my head. I jolted awake, gasping for air. The room spun and the threat of nausea trembled inside my throat, salivation building behind my tongue. Discomfort bellowed as an agonizing groan, an eerie sound crawling into a darkened room with no one to hear.

For a moment, I struggled to remember where I was, why I had no shirt on, and why I was sleeping sideways across the brown and tan upholstery stripes of a dirt-crusted motel chair. I lifted my twisted neck and wondered why someone would be ringing the doorbell to my room. And I wondered why the room even had a doorbell—motels have doorbells? My neck resisted straightening as I tried to sit, I encouraged it by wrapping my open palms around my head.

"Coming," I mumbled into the darkness, barely audible, residing just below the threshold of my pain.

Eyes barely open, I fumbled with the door chain, over and over, unable to get the chain to enter the track. I stopped when I realized the brass chain was already loose and dangling. I attempted to turn the deadbolt, but it was also already unlocked. It was then I realized I had, again, slept in this dirty cheap motel room with the door unlocked.

I opened the door and absorbed a blast of heat and light from the aggressive mid-morning sun. I lifted my hand to cover already squinted eyes in an attempt to prevent a nausea surge. I wasn't sure if I would succeed. I pressed my eyes shut with such pressure that a new wave of pain resonated gong-like back and forth between my ears.

"What?" I mumbled blindly out the door. When I heard no response, I growled louder, "What the hell do you want?"

I heard wind, I heard palm leaves rustling, I heard an out-of-tune truck engine sputtering in the distance, but I didn't hear anyone speak. I eased light into my eyes and peered through fingers to find a sparse parking lot baking in the morning heat, and my rental Jeep's flat windshield reflecting sunlight directly into my doorway.

I leaned forward, just enough to look left down the motel

face. Three doors away, a young boy stood on the sidewalk holding a stick like a sword. He spun and thrust with bent knees, all the while holding an open hand behind his back. He extended his stick forward with a quick jab and struck the room's doorbell button with impressive precision and form.

"Die!" he declared as he spun again to thrust toward an invisible opponent behind him.

"Sonofabitch," I mumbled to myself, *Kid Zorro's up early.*

Two doors beyond the boy was the motel cleaning cart lodged against the doorframe. I wasn't surprised to see the cleaning cart since Kid Zorro always accompanied his mother while she worked, but I was surprised because the presence of Miss Claire's cart revealed how much later in the morning it was than I had hoped.

Turning into the doorway, I noticed a paint-crusted doorbell protruding from the crumbling stucco facade next to my room.

A doorbell, I thought to myself, *Why is there a doorbell?*

I shut off the sunlight behind me, welcoming the soothing comfort of the dark. But as I shuffled toward the bed, the room spun and a surge of nausea rose within my throat to reach the back of my salivating tongue. Running into the bathroom, I expelled the high tide that had been taunting me since Kid Zorro's stabbing wakeup call.

When the contractions and gasping and spewing stopped, I fell back sitting and pressed my head against the wall as tears consumed my eyes. The soupy stench of stomach acid and alcohol slurried with the humid air. Then I realized I didn't lock the door. Miss Claire would be arriving shortly and the door was unlocked again.

• • •

THE GREEN DINER BENCH SQUEAKED AND GROANED as I sat and the cold seeped into the back of my legs. The excessive air conditioning was welcome therapy for my pounding head. I'd been eating supper at this diner for two weeks, but this was the first time I'd ordered breakfast and the first time I'd worn sunglasses inside. The diner was the subject of the most popular postcards received by loved ones for its throwback decor and the amount of chrome incorporated into everything that wasn't glass. This same chrome reflected every ray of the midday sun into my stabbing eyes.

Batya was a little more talkative than when I had seen her on previous evenings, perhaps because the diner was empty, or maybe because she knew it was my last day. She seemed excitable, laughing more than usual at something the unseen cook had said to her. She let him know he wouldn't get away with those words if the diner was busy, then burst into laughter again. I'm not sure what they were talking about and I really didn't care, I just wanted my eggs and toast—a pragmatic calm for an emotional stomach.

"I'm gonna miss you," Batya said cheerfully as she approached with a cup of coffee, "I hope you found what you came for."

I raised my eyebrows and grunted an ambiguous acknowledgment into the steam of my coffee. She remained standing next to my booth as I sipped, smiling that impish smile of hers which sat just in front of something clever she wanted to say. I returned the cup to its saucer and peered over the top of my sunglasses, "What?"

She shifted on her feet and crossed her arms, the smile growing wider, "Well, did you?"

"Did I what?"

"Find what you came for?"

I tilted my head to the side and forced my neck to crack, and with a slow blink I said, "I don't think so."

"You've still got time, you know."

"I leave today, time's up."

She laughed but covered her mouth to mute it, "How much time do you think you need?"

"I started with two weeks, and I've run down to zero. All done."

"Pancakes," she said as her smile relaxed.

"No thanks, I'd really just like my eggs and toast. How long does that take, anyway?"

"Be done in a minute. That's not what I meant."

My words slowed, "My head is pounding and easy to confuse, which you have accomplished. So please help me a little here."

"Pancakes, you just need to take him pancakes. He's a sucker for Roderigo's pancakes."

With minimal movement, I shook my head and attempted to restrain contempt, "I've spent two weeks looking and all of a sudden he'll appear for some pancakes? Okay," I said while lifting a sarcastic thumbs-up.

"All you had to do was ask, I would have told you. But you haven't come across as very approachable—a bit of an angry drunk later in the day, I'd say."

She wasn't wrong so I conceded, "Okay … okay. I haven't had the best focus here. Probably not the most welcomed guest in the diner."

"That's all right, I have faith in you," she said as she turned to weave behind the counter toward the plate which the unseen cook had just passed through from the grill. She grabbed the coffee pot on her way back.

"I think I'll have Roderigo make you up those pancakes. Can't have you leaving like this, unfulfilled and all."

She topped off my coffee while forming a smaller version of her smile. In a blink she was behind the counter, leaving the steam of my eggs swirling above the plate.

• • •

AS I EXTRACTED THE LAST CRUNCH from my toast, Batya
stood next to my table again, placing the check and a styrofoam carry-out container on the table. I picked up the check and
noticed she had added pancakes to my bill.

"Wait a minute, you're charging me for pancakes?"

"It's the best investment you'll ever make, for the price of
pancakes. I put three flavors of syrup inside, he likes to mix them
together."

I threw a skeptical gaze, but Batya returned an assuring nod.
I pulled out a small stack of folded bills from my front pocket and
removed a ten, paired it with the check, and extended my hand to
her. When she reached for it, I pulled back just out of her reach,
added another ten to the check, and said, "So how do I find him?"

She took the check and the two bills and laughed, then handed one of the tens back to me.

"Silly boy, he's down on the beach—should be taking a break
soon. He'll be quite pleased when you bring him this," she said as
she tapped the foam container.

"The beach? As you can see from my ripe strawberry skin,
I've been at the beach quite a bit … wasn't there."

"Not *that* beach … *this* beach," she said as she motioned out
the window to a sandy trail lined with ferns and palms leading
down the hill behind the diner.

"When did that get there?"

"You'd better get going."

• • •

THE SUN ROSE HIGH AND THE WIND coursed firm as I took
careful steps on the sandy path down toward the beach, the hill
encouraging my forward progress. Just past a large growth of tall
grass, the path spilled out onto a sandy bay—a beautiful beach
framed by large rocky outcrops a quarter mile in each direction.

The wind off the water was warm and humid. Its caress lifted and tossed my uncombed hair, fluttering it against my sunglasses.

Walking halfway to the water, I stopped and looked around. The beach was empty and completely void of footprints except for those leading up to the backs of my own shoes. The sun was centered above the half-moon shape of the bay, but the dancing shimmer on the water and my hangover made it painful to look outward. The waves seemed larger than I would have expected for this small bay, breaking as big as the pro surfing competition I watched in the airport bar.

I noticed a distant lone surfer near one of the rocks, but only after he popped up to stand on his board, knees bent and arms spread, weaving amongst the curving, crashing whitecaps of the water. He rode a cresting wave the entire length of the bay as if he commanded peasant water molecules to carry an esteemed royal prince.

I lost sight of the surfer when a wave crashed over his head and sent him tumbling. But then he emerged from the water carrying his board under his arm and headed right toward me. He beamed with excitement as he jogged, his smile wide and bright, his joyous eyes locked with mine. Long sun-bleached hair hugged the boyish skin of his butterscotch-toffee cheeks, draping along his neck and touching the tops of his wide shoulders.

When he reached me, he dropped his board and placed his hands on his hips.

"G'day my friend!" he said, excited words tainted with a heavy accent—some blend of Australian and perhaps South African—a pronounced distortion of vowels.

"The girl from the diner told me this is …" I said before realizing how silly I was about to sound, "that I should bring pancakes down to the beach. Honestly, I'm a little fuzzy on how this works."

"Batya?" he asked with a smile. He opened his hand to gesture toward the sandy path, "Batya from up top?"

The surfer had a twinkle in his eye that made me uncomfortable. I thought of the rich kids in my high school who spent two-week vacations skiing at expensive resorts while my sister and I felt lucky to get a trip to the Dairy Queen.

I hesitated before I said, "I'm not actually sure if you're who I'm looking for, she didn't say what you—I mean what he looks like."

"Batya told you how to find me, and you found me all right! This is what I look like." he proudly exclaimed while spreading his arms wide.

"No offense, but I thought God would be a little more … majestic."

He grabbed his jaw and a look of worry melted across his face. He fondled a wet clump of hair from his shoulder and brought it in front of his concerned eyes, "It's the hair … isn't it?" then broke into a big smile, "I can look however I want, friend. The big angry Zeus look was all right for a while, but this is way more fun," he said as he flexed a bicep, "and appropriate for my retirement lifestyle!"

I remembered the pancakes and extended the styrofoam container and said, "For you."

He held an unbroken gaze directly into my eyes as his smile remained wide, "Thank you so much," he said with remarkable calm, "I'm glad you stopped by."

With a gentle touch, he took the container and turned away, and collapsed to sit facing the waves with legs crossed. He placed the container onto his lap and lifted the lid in the most patient God-like way. He opened the three syrup containers, one at a time, and covered the pancakes with swirls of sticky brown, red, and blue.

"Perfect," he said.

He unwrapped the plastic utensils Batya had included and cut a bite-sized section from the stack of pancakes. Raising the fork in front of his face, he said to himself, "Roderigo, you're a genius," then began to eat.

I watched over his shoulder as he hummed with delight and closed his eyes with each bite. I was mesmerized watching him eat with such patience and joy, his satisfaction convincing me this just may have been the best meal he had ever eaten.

When finished, he placed the syrup cups and the utensils into the styrofoam container and closed the lid with the same patience he had shown while eating. After a few seconds of silence and no movement, I leaned forward over his shoulder to see his face and found him smiling with closed eyes.

"Sir?" I said in my most unassuming way.

In one continuous slow movement, he turned toward me and opened his eyes.

"G'day my friend!" he said as if we had never met.

"I'm not sure, but it seems like you maybe forgot I was here."

"Right! Thanks for the short stack, so very delicious," he said as he stood and handed me the styrofoam container.

He turned to look out to the water and formed a makeshift visor with his hand, "Man, did you see that? Perfect wave."

I looked at the waves but my inexperienced eyes saw nothing but random waves crashing and foaming into a dissipating mist.

"Sir," I began, "I came here looking to find, I guess, peace within myself. I was hoping to maybe find a meaningful relationship with God, one that's been missing for ... well, forever. I thought maybe ..."

"Really? That's quite nice of you," he said in his friendliest tone as he pointed toward another breaking wave, "Oh!"

I confessed, "This is not really how I thought things would go."

He turned to me and said, "How should things go, then? Didn't I tell you I'm retired?"

"You did mention that, I just thought when I found God ... I'd become filled with some enlightening purpose or ... something."

"Ah, I gotcha. You see, the thing is, shortly after I created everything and kind of got the ball rolling, there wasn't much for me to do. I'm really a hands-off type of guy."

"But people say they hear from you, and you guide them. So many people in the world insist you speak directly to them."

"Kinda silly if you think about it, isn't it?" he said with a sly smile and a wink.

"People dedicate their lives to you, spreading your words from the Bible."

"Those aren't my words, not my words at all. In fact, I've never once given an interview. And if I did, what I'd have to say would probably seem confusing—except maybe to surfers. And pancake lovers. Gods aren't so impressive whose words are '*Life gives you tasty waves, ride them out*' or '*Know which food makes your eyes roll back*' ... everyone wants there to be more to it than that."

He held up his palm.

"Sorry friend, not interested," he said before spreading his smile wide.

He picked up his board and jogged back toward the surf. I watched him enter the water and start paddling on his board but soon lost sight of him. With the shimmer of the water and the chaos of the waves, I never saw him again.

I made my way to the sandy path between the tall clumps of grass and climbed away from the beach. When I reached the top of the hill I was wheezing, my lungs were tight—insisting that I quit smoking. As I was bent over gasping for air, I could see Batya moving around in the otherwise empty diner, laughing at something the cook said.

I turned toward the parking lot and approached the only vehicle there, my rental Jeep. I climbed in and sat, placing the styrofoam container on the passenger floorboards.

"God's trash," I mumbled to myself. I was about to drive God's trash to the airport.

THE PROPELLORS OF THE TWIN-ENGINE airplane spun fast in preparation for takeoff. I could see cresting waves on the shoreline from my window as we accelerated down the runway.

I wished we could circle the island one time so I could try to find the diner. I knew it was on the south shore, but at that moment had trouble remembering exactly how to get there.

I wanted to try to spot God, to see him surfing and smiling in that half-moon bay between the rocky outcrops. I wanted more time but we were aimed right toward the mainland and destined for a straight, steady flight path.

• • •

LIFE HAS HANDED ME SOME challenges in the years since that trip, but I like to think of them as tasty waves thrown at me by life; temporary turbulence I attack with bent knees, spread arms, and an undefeatable smile.

It's been years since my drunken friends assured me that I was incapable of finding spiritual enlightenment. They said I was incorrigible and promised that they would one day come to visit me in prison. I bet them a round of drinks that all I needed was two weeks and a warm island and I could prove them wrong.

When I returned, I admitted failure and bought everyone drinks that night. The sounds of clinking glasses and impaired singing filled the pub and I let them all laugh at my defeat and mock my gullible proposal of the bet. I told them how drunk I would get and how I kept leaving the motel door unlocked. I told them how the motel inexplicably had a doorbell outside every room. I told them how Kid Zorro could stab a mosquito right out of the air.

But what I didn't tell them, is that for the price of pancakes, I met God on a beach. And that I left his trash—and my own, too—behind at the airport.

ROOMS OF RUBY AND PEARL

ELAINE SANFORD EASED AWAKE as the swaying of the carriage softened and the rhythmic thumping of the horses slowed from a canter to a trot. The driver announced from above that they were now approaching the Grand Hotel and a porter would be tending to her travel bag upon arrival. The estate came into view and its grandiose beauty induced a gasp from Miss Sanford.

This clearly had once been a majestic cathedral with its baroque spires and stained glass. The stone chimera and grotesques were as pristine as the day they were carved. The Hotel seemed to float on an island of lush green landscaping with a perfect design of shrubs and trees. An overwhelming cascade of fruity and spicy aromas filled the carriage as it passed a field of elegant blooming flowers.

The temperature was pleasant and the skies cloudless as Miss Sanford stepped down onto the white pebbles of the carriageway. She ambled forward in awe to the base of an enormous staircase leading up to the majestic entrance of Roman pillars and magnificent arches.

Feeling disheveled and humbled to be standing in front of such splendor and glory, she brushed the dust off her blouse sleeves and tucked wily strands of butterscotch hair behind her ears.

THE LOBBY FLOOR OF THE GRAND HOTEL was paved in Italian marble, with feathery gray veins weaving through the glistening alabaster stone. Larger-than-life sculptures of Roman gods carved from the finest Carrara marble rested atop mighty pedestals. The row of gods peered down as resolute guardians of all who passed, prompting Miss Sanford to bow her head in humility.

The front desk clerk was unwavering in her pleasantries, her perfect posture and genuine smile were calm and warming. Her mauve jacket was pinned with a fresh white chrysanthemum and she welcomed her new guest with sincerity. As Miss Sanford stood with windblown hair, perspiry skin, and a distant gaze, the clerk asked how her travels had been on such a wonderful day.

Miss Sanford apologized profusely for her condition. She admitted she was quite fatigued and must have fallen victim to sleepiness early on for she was having a bit of trouble remembering details of her trip.

The clerk assured Miss Sanford the long carriage journey up the mountain, coupled with the altitude of the Grand Hotel, could often produce such fatigue. She added that the hotel's world-class dining facilities would assuredly bring Miss Sanford back to true form in no time and asked if she had a time preference for dinner.

"Oh, wonderful, thank you, I am quite famished. I shall need thirty minutes to freshen up. Please reserve a table for one, if it's not too much trouble."

The clerk nodded and said, "Of course it's not."

She stated that upon Miss Sanford's return from her room, she should make her way to the opposite end of the lobby and announce herself to the maître d'. The clerk assured her a table would be ready, as the dining facilities were expecting her visit.

Miss Sanford doubly thanked the clerk and headed for the elevator lift.

FREDERICK HOLLAND ENTERED THE HOTEL with an aggressive gait and passed Miss Sanford in front of the pedestal supporting the enormous Jupiter sculpture. Mister Holland pinched the knot of his tie, adjusted his gold cufflinks, and cleared his throat with haughty volume. Straightening his fedora while scanning the lobby, he mumbled to himself that it was not the worst shack he'd ever stayed in.

The front desk clerk welcomed Mister Holland with unwavering pleasantries and asked how his travels had been on such a wonderful day.

"Well, doll, I wish I could say everything's dandy," he said as he tossed his dusty hat onto the counter, "but the warmness of the carriage ride must have caused me to nod off. I'm feeling a bit foggy, you hear me? You'd think the livery could do a better job with their important customers."

The clerk acknowledged the air may have felt warmer than he was expecting, and reiterated the tendency for the journey to sap a fine traveler's energy, even one with the hearty constitution of Mister Holland. She insisted that the upward trip was all behind him now and he should look forward to dinner at the hotel's world-class dining facilities.

Mister Holland stated that he needed a change of suit and to put a good splash on his face. He expected he'd be back down in thirty minutes.

The clerk thanked Mister Holland and said that upon his return, he should make his way to the opposite end of the lobby and announce himself to the maître d', who would then take care of him.

He cleared his throat and swiped up his hat from the counter.

"Hey gal," he scoffed, "what's with all the ancient decor?

"Nobody believes in these gods anymore—you should modernize the place."

"Thank you, Mister Holland, I will pass your message on to management," the clerk said with a smile.

Mister Holland's brash expression melted into disgust and he turned from the counter.

"Who hires these stiff dames?" he mumbled as he strode away.

WHEN A REFRESHED MISS SANFORD returned to the elevator for dinner, Mister Holland was inside and heading to the lobby as well. He stood wide in the center of the car, but shifted on his feet and sighed at the inconvenience of the stop.

They both had cleaned up and changed into new attire for dining. The expensive suit Mister Holland had worn on his incoming trip had been replaced with an even more expensive suit. His wingtip shoes had been wiped clean of the trip's dust, bringing back the shine he had procured in the city.

In stark contrast, Miss Sanford's change of clothes was a modest gray dress draped with a loose black shawl. Mister Holland indiscreetly inspected Miss Sanford from shoes to shoulders and snickered. He asked her why she dressed so dull within the walls of the Grand Hotel. He stroked his lapels and bragged about his indecision of which suit in his wardrobe made him look best. Miss Sanford stated uncomfortably that she was a school teacher and a woman of modest means and the facilities would certainly have no issue with her wardrobe.

Mister Holland looked down his nose and sniffed and asked if she was one of those unrestrained women causing all the latest trouble—one of those ridiculous new suffragettes. Miss Sanford stated with conviction that she was indeed supportive of women and their rights, and that pompous patronizing men, such as himself, will one day seek employment from a superior woman, such as herself.

As the elevator doors opened, Mister Holland's laughter echoed through the lobby. Miss Sanford set forth in disgusted haste to meet her committed reservation time. Mister Holland strolled at a casual pace and announced to the lobby that he could not believe the words spoken by this callow mistress. He motioned up to the statue of Libertas and said, "Do you believe that dame?"

MISS SANFORD POLITELY INTRODUCED herself to the maître d' and asked if a table was still available.

Dressed in a crisp white tuxedo, he said, "Very lovely to have you, Miss Sanford. I see the Grand Hotel has pre-assigned your dining to the Pearl Room, it will be perfect for such a graceful woman as yourself. Occupancy is very low today."

A young tuxedo-clad boy escorted Miss Sanford up one flight of stairs and held open the door to the Pearl Room.

Arriving at the maître d' shortly after Miss Sanford, Mister Holland announced himself using his long, self-important business title. He added that perhaps the hotel could up its game a little.

"Ain't been much grand about it so far, pal," he said.

The maître d' said, "Ah, Mister Holland, we've been expecting you. I see the hotel has pre-assigned you to the Ruby Room, it will be perfect for a man with your credentials."

Mister Holland nodded in smug agreement, then was struck dumbfounded as he raised a finger and asked why there were two dining facilities with the low traffic he had observed in the lobby.

The maître d' explained that dining occupancy can be wildly inconsistent and that the hotel assigns patrons to the two different dining rooms based on their reputation and disposition. The Ruby Room is reserved for guests who are outwardly more vigorous in their expectations of fellow cohorts. A patron of bellicose spirit, such as Mister Holland, is a good indicator of a Ruby Room guest.

"What's the other one?" Mister Holland asked.

"The Pearl Room is for those of a different moral standing, those without that Ruby Room fire in their soul."

"That's right," said Mister Holland, "I'm a Ruby Room type of fellow. No place for me in the humdrum Pearl Room, the way I see it."

The maître d' smiled and said, "I couldn't agree more."

The tuxedo-clad boy escorted Mister Holland down one flight of stairs and held open the door to the Ruby Room.

MISS SANFORD ENTERED THE PEARL room and stood on the white marble reception floor. The ceiling was high and the room was pleasantly illuminated with several large crystal chandeliers sparkling in the sunshine. Flowing silk drapes adorned clear windows with wonderful views of the blue sky. The air was filled with the delicious aroma of steaks and seafood, and of fresh bread and garlic. Miss Sanford closed her eyes and inhaled a deep breath. A string quartet sat on a raised platform and played a sonata from Miss Sanford's favorite classical composer.

She stepped up to the host stand with a big smile and couldn't restrain her delight. "My goodness, this is so wonderful," she exclaimed.

"Elaine, welcome. We've been expecting you," the smiling host said as he escorted Miss Sanford to her table. Resting upon a white tablecloth, a fine silver place setting shimmered with reflections of the chandeliers above.

"Your table. Enjoy."

Miss Sanford sat and was immediately served the first course of Duck à l'orange, a dish she had once ordered while dining with her late father. In celebration of her sixteenth birthday, he had taken her to a fancy French restaurant in the city, and that special meal had remained one of her favorite memories of him.

She whispered to herself, "So lovely, so heavenly."

Across the room, Miss Sanford noticed a young girl, still just a child, being served a chocolate-covered eclair. The girl emitted a certain joy and purity that reminded Miss Sanford of a former student who had fallen ill and never returned to school. A tear formed in Miss Sandford's eye as she watched the girl's angelic smile.

MISTER HOLLAND ENTERED THE RUBY room and found himself pressed into a crowd of patrons waiting to be seated. The men were sweaty and rank, and the women were so overly-perfumed that Mister Holland had trouble breathing. The ceiling was low and the room was dimly lit with candles that flickered intermittently within dirty sconces on the walls.

In the shadowed corner of the waiting area, a pair of men wearing tall hats played out-of-tune bagpipes at such an excruciating volume that Mister Holland lifted his hands to cover his ears. Every few seconds a new patron would press into the waiting crowd and cause a wave of flailing elbows and stuttering feet.

Mister Holland raised his voice and yelled at a man next to him, "This is horrible. What's the wait—how long have you been waiting?"

"It seems like months," the man yelled back, "it just keeps getting more crowded without anyone being seated."

Mister Holland pushed his way through the crowd to the host stand, but no one was tending to it. He looked across the tables of seated patrons and found that none of them had been served any food or drink. Many were pounding on the tables and yelling at each other.

Mister Holland reached into his vest pocket to check the time but found his watch missing.

"Hey!" he screamed across the crowd, "Which one of you cretins stole my watch, huh? It's worth more than all of you combined!"

The bagpipes continued to send a painful shrill through Mister Holland's head as a man with a red bow tie and pencil-thin mustache appeared at the stand and tapped on the reservation list.

Smiling with a condescending sneer, the host said, "Frederick Holland, we've been expecting you. Please wait at the back of the queue, please."

Mister Holland raised his voice above the noise, "Hey, Jack, this dining room is miserable, I want out of here—how do I get into to the Pearl Room?"

"You don't," he said.

Mister Holland shouted back, "Look, I've only been here five minutes but it seems like an eternity. What kind of hellish place is this?"

The host laughed before he said, "Calling the Ruby Room Hell-*ish* is rather naive and boorish of you, sir."

He twisted the tip of his mustache and smiled.

"An eternity of misery? That's kind of the point now, isn't it?"

MAD HOUSE

I PURCHASED THIS LITTLE HOUSE for quite a bargain, without negotiation. The old man who lived here passed on and his daughter was anxious to sell. She mentioned that he had stopped leaving the house and was having memory lapses and hallucinations. She said his condition worsened rather suddenly and it may have been the complete isolation that drove him mad. In my opinion, madness is a rather outdated, comprehensive diagnosis of days gone by. Surely he was merely— and quite simply—just old.

One feature that drew me to this house was the small, windowless room in the back of the basement. Quite unassuming and barely useful, this room will fulfill what I need: a space to isolate and create. Most painters desire an open space, copious lighting, and a scene of abundant sensory stimulation as their muse. But not me. I plan to spend a lot of time here in this house, in the quiet, in this room.

I've spent a lengthy career bound to the university, held tightly within the safe arms of a tenure appointment. I endured it to the end, but now I'm retired from that madhouse. Some people say you should never retire or you'll lose yourself and your sanity.

But I might argue that remaining an educator in an environment of hedonism and hangovers is what will really test your sanity. I'm free now, free from the demons that have been feeding my resentment and tainting my brain with disdain for the very students I'm supposed to care about. It's time to let my inner beast out.

I'VE BEEN HERE FOR TWO weeks. My possessions are simple and already organized upstairs. In my creative isolation room, my easel is set up and paints are arranged on a small table to my side. My singular light source is a black swing-arm desk lamp, positioned not far from my cheek. Fitted with a low-wattage bulb, it illuminates my tools and the patient canvas. I need not see anything else to work—isolation will feed my muse.

I've decided tonight's composition will be a wooded landscape. I brush an even distribution of Manganese Cerulean across the canvas, a perfect springtime sky. With the base layer of paint applied, the balsamic smell reassures me that change is in the air, something beautiful will be created out of nothingness.

As I ponder which shades of green trees inspire me at this moment—midwest oaks and elms, or southeast pines and Bradford Pears—a heavy metallic crash startles me from outside my sanctuary doorway.

"Michaela!" I bellow.

Normally, she would lounge on pillows and window sills, her immutable feline predator genes watching garden visitors. But I suppose this house has introduced new interests, new places to wander, new places to pounce and piss. Admittedly, I probably left the basement door open.

I lift a metal painting knife for mixing my greens. I've decided on midwest. I scan over my paints to locate the necessary hues.

With a piercing slap of wood to the concrete floor, a broom falls with unusual force.

"Michaela!" I bluster again.

I grab the hood of the lamp and turn it toward the door-way, casting a faint wash of light on the fallen broom. I squint to look for Michaela, but she eludes me. I rotate the lamp further to reveal abstract stains and scratches on the concrete walls. I catch a glimpse of a shimmer in the silver handle of an abandoned bucket. And there seems to be a shadow looming on the wall with nothing to cast it.

"Michaela, out!" I command.

I can't see her, nor do I hear any movement. I move the anemic light across the doorway and broom again before rotating the lamp back.

As I turn to continue painting, my canvas has been disrupted with a sloppy, solid oval of Cadmium Red. Startled, I glance at my brushes to find none wet with this color. I should certainly remember applying it, but my sense of time seems to be stretching and contracting tonight. I study the eerie shape further and discover the subtleties of a face with no eyes, crude but with hints of facial features. I wrap my fingers around the paint knife, a tighter grip driven by tightening nerves. At my age, I shouldn't be afraid of the dark, yet here I sit trembling.

As I reach to pull the lamp hood closer, my table of paints overturns from underneath with a loud crash. I nearly fall off my stool. I direct the lamp to the upended table and see nothing but scattered paints and brushes. I scan the floor between the table and the doorway and find no sign of Michaela or the broom.

I become completely still listening for movement in the room, listening for paws or vocalizations, listening for anything at all. But, as before, there is only silence.

The faint shadow on the wall seems to morph from an unshapen stain into a silhouette, and back again. Then it moves—at first like an old man with a cane, then as a child chasing a balloon. It stops and becomes indiscernible for a moment before launching off the wall toward me.

I rotate the lamp to follow the shadow and find the disruption on my canvas is now fully featured and grinning. I'm staring into a horrible face, a face of fright and terror—vile red skin with jaundiced yellow eyes, curved horns protruding from a shiny forehead, and sharp teeth encased in an evil smile.

I gasp. My heart races—eyes widen—hands shake.

A humid, rancid breath caresses the back of my ear. A rumbling growl sends tingles across my neck. I lift my eyes to the lamp, my hand still grasping it. The growl becomes stronger, seeming to disapprove of my thoughts.

I conclude the grotesque image on the canvas is a self-portrait of the owner of that gurgling growl, and I have no desire to see this deathly thing in any form—painted or living.

Wrapping my fingers tightly around the knife, I plunge it into the center of the painting, piercing the canvas between those horrific eyes.

A loud shriek of pain tears through my ear; a tremendous growl heats the air and weaves through my head. In the rush to cover my ears, I knock the lamp to the floor.

When the horrible howling and growling finally stops, I release my ears and restore the lamp, turning its hood toward the canvas again. There is no Cadmium Red, no face, no eyes—only Manganese Cerulean with my painter's knife protruding from the center.

I take a deep breath and touch my still-ringing ear.

I reach for the knife and ease it out of the canvas. I inspect its paint-free sterility, then drop it to the pile of strewn paints.

I close my eyes and rub my forehead as I take a much deeper breath.

As I regain focus, a drop of red paint forms where the canvas is cut. I lean in for a closer look, it's Crimson, I believe. The small drop becomes a trickle and it creeps down the canvas. I stop it with the side of my finger. Immediately upon my touch, the flow surges through the cut, and thick gobs of red cascade down—Crimson and Naphthol and Sanguine. I instinctively cup my hands together to capture it.

My hands overflow with the viscous liquid. To my surprise, it's quite warm. I slide my thumbs across my curved fingers and find the sensation quite scintillating, quite exciting. I laugh with joy. The warmth penetrates my hands and soothes my arthritic fingers. I wipe a slippery handful onto each forearm, and I feel its energy absorb into my body. I smear the canvas with my palms and fingers, forming a large, beautiful oval of infinite unity.

Electrical impulses jolt through my soul as surging flashes of color fill my eyes. All inhibition has left me, replaced with absolute freedom.

I collect more of the luscious, flowing heaven and bring it to my lips. It's sweet, it's warm, it's wonderful and delicious. I drink in this lifeblood, and I pulse with power, I pulse with its infinite power.

I dance around and hug the walls of my wonderful, isolated space of no inhibition where I can create, and where I can be created.

I have been rewarded and awakened, I shall slumber no more!

My aged bodily vessel is merely a constricting container, prohibiting inevitable unbounded evolution.

I begin to glow from within and cast my internal light throughout the room. Bright beams emanate from my fingertips and eyes. I have opened Jacob's Ladder!

With a wave of my hand, I create a portal for angels and demons to come together and be free to mingle and merge. I grant them unlimited power, for they will serve unto me in all my celestial glory!

· · ·

MY FOGGY HEAD RESTS AGAINST THE COLD concrete floor. My joints ache and my muscles throb. Michaela sits before me in silhouette, glaring with unimpressed hunger. I'm slow to rise, but with time I reach a stable sitting position.

A pristine canvas of evenly distributed Manganese Cerulean waits upon my easel beneath the faint glow of my spotlight. I can't recall how it got there, I must have painted it. It's beautiful. Perhaps it will make a wonderful Caribbean scene.

Michaela will have to wait a little while longer. I'm not certain of the time or day, but I'm in my fulfilling space, my space of isolation and sensory deprivation, and I can't delay getting started any longer.

My muse is calling. I must let it out.

OFF BY ONE

$$\rule{4cm}{0.4pt}$$

MY LITTLE SISTER DIED today.

While at work this morning, I received a call from my old friend Shondra. She sounded scared and asked if I had been watching the launch. I told her I wasn't.

"Seen one, you've seen 'em all," I said.

One of the accounting balances was off by one and I was having trouble finding the problem. I'm pretty good with math, but this particular audit had become quite an irritation.

Shondra told me there was an explosion, that during launch the whole ship blew up into a huge fireball, and all of the crew were lost.

Veteran astronaut LaTorie Jackson, my little sister, was on that ship.

* * *

FROM AN EARLY AGE, LaTorie was quirky and soft-spoken, but we were bound as both best friends and sisters. I would have given up my world for her. When she started school, I waited with her until her bus arrived. It meant that I would have to run as fast as I could to catch my own bus three blocks away, but it was important to me to make sure she got on the bus safely. It was quite an inconvenience, but I would have never left her alone there.

Mom and Dad were wonderful and always gave us great focus and love. Dad was playful and optimistic, with a great smile, and would often proclaim with excitement, "The Jackson Sisters are gonna change the world!"

Mom was more level-headed and pragmatic. She often reminded us that we still had to do our homework, even if it was always too easy. She would motion toward Dad and say, "You can't change the world when you skirt your responsibilities."

To which he would reply, "That's right, listen to Momma."

Math and science were my love, but LaTorie operated on a different level. It was hard to tell what interested her most because everything was interesting to her, and she was good at all of it. And she didn't speak much.

We learned the importance of phrasing when communicating with LaTorie. You couldn't ask her something like '*Would you like to help me with dinner?*' because she would say '*No*'. The effective way was to say '*Please help me with dinner*', and she would say '*Okay*'.

SOMETIMES ON THE WEEKENDS, we walked over to the neighbor's farm to sit on a broken fence and watch the cows. I liked to analyze the architecture of the barns and think about how the field layouts could be better optimized for crop rotation. I thought of the Fence Post Problem and the off-by-one errors that many of my classmates struggled with.

We named the cows after their physical traits. Doughnut had a big spot of two concentric circles. White Ear was completely black except for one ear.

LaTorie noticed variances in their behavioral patterns, "Ohio used to wait for Elvis to drink first," she once pointed out, "but now she doesn't wait for anyone."

Sometimes LaTorie only stared toward the sky, lost in deep thought about something atmospheric, or perhaps something even further into the cosmos.

She had a unique focus when analyzing an object, a pattern, or even just a moment in time. Even when she was very young she stared, unblinking, consumed by that particular moment. I learned that regardless of any of my own boredom or urgencies, I just needed to wait for her to finish. She wouldn't respond to anything I'd say while deep in her focus, so regardless of much frustration, I became good at patience. Patience was a good thing to master with LaTorie.

OF COURSE, THE OTHER KIDS at school found her an easy target for teasing and would say things like, "When they handed out brains, they must have skipped this one!" or chant over and over, "Dumb, dumb, off by one!"

One time when I gave Pigpen Pryor a fat lip, Mom and Dad made it clear that participating in a fight over immature words was not worth the outcome. Even though the teasing left me unsettled and prepared to engage and defend her, LaTorie never acknowledged any of it.

TWO WEEKS AFTER I GRADUATED from high school, my parents left for an anniversary trip to drive around Europe. It was a surprise gift for Mom, but since she was much better at planning details than Dad, I helped him with the logistics.

They had never really taken a big trip together, so Dad wanted to make the most of it and get maximum value out of his limited budget. I helped optimize their travel route using algorithms from the Traveling Salesman problem. It was well-planned and they were both excited.

Since I had already turned eighteen, they felt comfortable leaving us alone while they were gone. They made sure their wills were up to date and even appointed me executor of their estate in case there were any problems.

There were problems.

Shortly after landing in London, they were involved in a fatal car crash. This was devastating and left me an emotional wreck for a long time. LaTorie never externalized much about it, but I think over time she became as crushed as I was. Only once, a few years later, did I ever see her cry.

For the upcoming fall semester, I had been offered a full-ride engineering scholarship to MIT in Boston, but school had to be put on hold. Now that I was the legal guardian of LaTorie, there was no way I could do anything but take on responsibility as her caregiver.

I had worked two summers at the local grocery store and was able to get hired back as a cashier. They were flexible and let me work hours that permitted proper time to care for LaTorie. It wasn't a terrible job, but being a cashier is kind of boring. I played a game where I could look at a customer's items and add up the prices in my head before I even scanned a single milk carton.

It was difficult seeing my ex-classmates come home for breaks and overhear about how great college was going. I itched to be there with them. But making sure LaTorie had a solid home and a good future was important to me.

I stayed with the company until LaTorie graduated from school. By that time, I had garnered the attention of corporate and was working as a senior accountant in the main office.

LaTorie went on to excel at aeronautical engineering and rose to prominence in the international space program. Early on, I was a little envious of her accomplishments, but I had become tired. The six years of raising her alone were hard on me and really dulled my excitement about going back to college. I had made a comfortable place for myself at corporate and remained living in our old house, it was my home. Old resentments faded over time, and I became quite proud of her.

• • •

WHEN SHONDRA CALLED this morning, she added that in anticipation of this historic launch, she had pulled LaTorie's academic files in case news reporters came around asking questions about LaTorie's time here. Shondra works for the school district and has access to former students' records.

"I was looking at her records and saw something I never knew," she whispered into the phone, "LaTorie had the second highest score on the aptitude testing, across the whole state. *Ever!*"

I didn't know how to respond.

She continued, "Okay, so that made me curious, and you know what else I found? She was the second-highest score by only one point. Off by only one!"

I was pretty shaken from the overwhelming news, and exhausted from the flood of memories, but I continued to listen with patience.

"Wanna know what *else* I found?" she whispered, "Okay, ready for this? Do you know who was the top score, who was the number one to LaTorie?"

I knew the answer, but said, "No."

Shondra paused before saying, "You were."

I HUNG UP WITH SHONDRA and shut down my computer. I left work and drove over to the old farm to sit on a broken fence and look at cows and mourn.

For the remainder of today, the company's accounting error will remain, like the Jackson sisters, off by one.

AUBURN ANGEL

I N 1973 I LOST A TOWN. IT WAS my favorite town of those I had never visited. And most towns were ones I had never visited since my parents never took us anywhere. Occasionally we would leave the suburbs and drive into the very flat countryside. We'd pass through endless cornfields and a few tiny Amish villages to spend the weekend at my uncle's farm. But we never went to my favorite town.

Dreaming of a cherished place is understandable for a 12-year-old, and I wouldn't be surprised if other kids chose Orlando or Wisconsin Dells. But theirs are likely ones they had visited. Not mine. Mine was a place I had only read about.

My dad was passionate about reading. Breakfast was consumed with a lit cigarette and an open paperback. Our basement bookcase was overflowing and a dirty gold recliner sat like a throne in front of his bound paper kingdom. He didn't care where his books came from, he'd find thrifty ways to acquire them—the county flea market, bookstore sidewalk sales, and even the library discount bin.

I remember the day he brought home a full set of the 1957 World Book encyclopedias. I was home for summer break and reading a new comic book on the couch. He arrived with two produce boxes and stacked them near the bookcase. He pulled off as many books as necessary from the lowest shelf to clear about two feet of space. Then he unpacked.

Every volume was bound in textured leather the color of a blue summer's day sky. Golden embossed letters rose up the spines to broadcast the section of the alphabet contained within each respective book. The set was worn and every corner was dented or crushed and the page edges were filthy. And although they were fifteen years old, those books were a beautiful sight.

They exposed me to the expanse of our world—the reptiles, minerals, and planets that I would gain more detail about inside future classrooms. I would get completely lost in those books. I'd finish one book and pull the next from the shelf and read it like it was fine literature. Each subject entry was a fascinating snapshot of a tiny piece of our world, with words smart and intentional— yet never pretentious.

This was how I found my favorite town: Delgado Pass, Arizona. Book number 4 contained all of letter D and was one of the thinnest in the set. I liked the feel of the thinner books when I read while reclining on the couch. The heaviness of the big books made it harder to keep them upright for comfortable reading. Those big boys got consumed lying stomach-down on the floor, leaning on sore elbows.

The D book had three oversaturated photos of Delgado Pass, all with the brown and green off-color tint common for that pub- lication era. And they were shiny. Each was covered with a spot finish application of glossy varnish.

The first photo was an aerial view from high above show- ing Delgado Pass nestled like a beautiful heirloom broach in the cleavage of two magnificent mountain ranges.

The second photo was of the historic downtown, a stylized faux version of an old wild west town. Wooden plank sidewalks and unused hitching posts waited outside storefronts. A narrow building with wide bars over the windows bore a giant sign with the word *Jail*. The mountains rose with majestic authority behind the roof of a two-story hotel. A man stood in front of an authentic saloon's swinging doors, confidently boasting a bright red shirt with white fringe on the chest and forearms. His exaggerated smile was as white as his cowboy hat, which had certainly never seen a dusty ranch.

The third photo showed a happy family enjoying a picnic near a blossoming magnolia tree. All so perfect; a mother, father, and young boy sat on a red and white checkered blanket. A woven wicker picnic basket and four small plates sat between them. And they were all laughing at the world's corniest joke. But closer to the camera, resting on the seat of a swing with her calves extended and toes pointed, was the most beautiful girl I had ever seen.

A bright smile plumped her cheeks into dimples and perfect auburn hair was pulled back into a neat ponytail. A white sweater complemented her pink poodle skirt. Black and white saddle shoes hugged her perfect and proper feet. She was a hip teenager from the 1950s and I was unapologetically mesmerized. The encyclopedia entry of this tiny mountain town had not only given me a romanticized view of a wild west town, it fused the auburn-haired angel from the swing into my heart.

My dad once noticed that the D book was often missing from the shelf and asked me what was keeping me so fascinated. I lied and told him I loved the images of dynamite exploding away bedrock to lay a path for new railroads. He agreed that the early architects of westward expansion were pretty ingenious. He laughed for a moment before pointing a dead-serious finger, *don't play with dynamite*.

But the only thing related to railroads on my mind was the hope that one day I could arrive in Delgado Pass on a wooden passenger car pulled by an old black steam engine with billowing smoke. And when my foot left the last step, I would see the auburn-haired girl and she would smile at me and we would share a malted milkshake at the town's ice cream parlor as birds chirped in the sunshine.

My favorite fantasy played over and over in my head, and this fantasy cemented Delgado Pass as my favorite town.

• • •

THE NEXT YEAR IN SCHOOL my literature teacher occasionally allocated time to visit the school library during class. To my great surprise, I found they had purchased the brand new 1973 edition of the World Book. The pages were clean and the corners were sharp—quite different from my dented and dirty books at home.

I stood in front of the complete set and stared at the D book. The overly loud juvenile giggles in the neighboring aisles faded into silence. I had never seen newer editions of the World Book and didn't know what to expect. I wondered if the girl on the swing would be older in the photo now. I wondered if maybe she had been replaced with someone different. Maybe they added even more photos. My breath became shallow and my palms began to sweat.

I looked down the aisle to my left, then right. I was alone. I reached for the book and nestled my fingertip into the front pages like I had done so many times before at home. I eased the leather covers apart and opened to the entry for Delhi, India. I had performed this motion so many times on my own D book that I knew Delgado Pass was on the preceding page. I became frozen with anticipation—I felt like I was about to open the diary in Mom's nightstand. Maybe I shouldn't be using school time to look at my favorite town and fawn over the love of my life.

I scanned the aisle again, it would be a life-crushing embarrassment to get caught admiring a girl in front of my classmates. No one was near. I put pressure on the page and slid.

My heart sunk. There was no entry for Delgado Pass.

This can't be right, I thought.

I flipped the pages to check alphabetical order but there was no entry to be found. My favorite town was gone. Sweat formed in my armpits and I felt dizzy. Something felt wrong about this—something very, very wrong.

WHEN DAD GOT HOME THAT NIGHT, I stood waiting for him in the kitchen. I disguised my urgency by leaning against the sink drinking a glass of milk mixed with powdered Ovaltine. I asked him if World Book ever changes the information in their books.

"I suppose," he said as he loosened his necktie. "Things change all the time so they need to keep the books up to date. I'd imagine they get bigger every year."

"Would they ever just remove something ... like erase it?" I asked.

He stroked his chin as he pondered the question, "Unlikely."

Peeling the cellophane off a new pack of cigarettes, he said, "The names of countries sometimes change, so that would get an update. They'd create a new entry and move the information there. But they'd tell you how to find it."

He placed a new cigarette between his lips, it bobbled as he spoke, "And anything that goes extinct—like the Dodo or Tasmanian Tiger—will still be there, but with updated wording."

His analysis seemed right, but nowhere in the school's edition did it say Delgado Pass could be found under a different name or that it had gone extinct. And it would be impossible to flip through every page in the library's full set trying to spot the three photos from my books.

On my next class trip to the library, I headed to the card catalog and located the drawer where I was certain to find Delgado Pass. The cards gave up nothing. I switched drawers to search for *Arizona* and found a few travel guides and a giant volume titled *Historic Arizona*. Not a single one of these books made any mention of Delgado Pass.

SATURDAY MORNINGS MEANT DAD had two stops to make—the bank and the public library. For the first time that year, I went with him. The library had the same information on Delgado Pass as my school: absolutely nothing. I was irritated and confused. The thought that my favorite town and favorite girl could simply disappear with no discoverable trace left a small hole in my life—an internalized depression that stayed with me for decades.

• • •

HIGH SCHOOL SERVES AS THE TIME for kids to develop their identity, to be shaped and molded into their future selves. In the mid-'70s they did it in bellbottom jeans with sewn-on flower patches. The boys wore the same long hairstyles as the girls and the practice of shampooing was still waning from the previous decade. I found the smell and the sloppiness of these years unsettling. I hated the Viet Nam war and all the political reasons we had been there. And I hated its ongoing cultural repercussions still shaping my impressionable and malleable generation.

I didn't identify with my classmates at all. I didn't share an interest in the things they found entertaining. To some, a fun Friday night meant meeting at the football game—a time to look foolish and flirt with each other at the concession stand beside the bleachers. To others, it meant lounging in their cool friend's unkempt room and listening to *Hotel California* or *2112* with incense burning and a blacklight glowing.

But to me, a fun Friday night was spent visiting the library to browse the writings of Salinger and Hemingway and Bradbury; authors who represented a much better time.

The photos of Delgado Pass were washed with the purity of the 1950s. The family on their picnic was happy—the wide smiles were incontrovertible proof. The girl on the swing was so fresh and tightly crafted, that she would have been revolted by the dirtiness of the hippie culture. She would have wanted me to protect her from it—to turn down the fuzzbox guitars so we could enjoy our conversation.

I never stopped longing for her, the perfect girl from a perfect time.

• • •

COLLEGE COINCIDED WITH A NUDGE BACK toward conservatism. Dirt was out—clean was back. But even with that relief, the laziness of my peers left me unimpressed. I saw little point in expending social energy on them. I was still curious and studious like I had been years before while sitting in front of my dad's basement bookcase. He had led by great example.

Of course, my university library was void of evidence of Delgado Pass too—I checked it out my first week on campus. I became submerged in school work, but never forgot about the girl on the swing. Each year I took a spring break trip by myself. I'd choose a large city within a nine-hour driving distance. With a map unfolded on the front seat, I'd plan a route intersecting as many small towns as I could until I reached a halfway point. Then I'd lodge at a small motel and continue to the remaining half of the towns on the following day.

In every one of these small towns, I had a strict agenda. I'd perform a calculated search at the local library, then browse a small bookstore or two, and perhaps—if there was one—scan through an antique shop for old geography items. I'd find all kinds of books and maps of Arizona, but nowhere was a trace that Delgado Pass had ever existed. I found discarded encyclopedia sets—some as old as 1962—but my favorite town was missing from all of them. The only useful information I compiled was that at some point between 1957 and 1962, Delgado Pass was erased from history.

DURING THE LAST FEW WEEKS before graduation, I visited the

history department of my university. The department chair met me on a Friday afternoon under the promise that I had the most interesting problem he might ever solve. I described what I knew about Delgado Pass. I described all the places I *didn't* find information. I asked if he or any of the history staff could help me solve this never-ending mystery.

He listened patiently with an elbow on the desk and a hand across his mouth. When I finished sharing my story, he stood and turned toward the window. He squinted and furrowed his brow and fixed his eyes on something far away.

After a long pause, he sat back down and said, "When mid-eighteen-hundred gold rush towns were abandoned, evidence has lasted to this day. When ancient civilizations fell, evidence of their existence lasted for millennia—and still stands. What I think you're speaking about, is evidence of something much different—a published prank you've become obsessed with. Nothing more."

"No—no, that's not true. This town existed. I saw it—I saw the pictures in that 1957 encyclopedia. There were three photos and the town was very much real!"

Nervously rubbing his palms together, he said, "You're mistaken."

He shook his head several times before stopping his eyes on the desk phone. He leaned toward me and whispered, "Do you still have the book?"

His look had completely transformed. There was something much more serious and deeply unnerving about his eyes.

"No, I … I … don't," I said with caution, "it's been a long time since I've seen it."

He sighed and reached for the phone, but stopped short of touching it. He rested his palm on the desk and tapped his index finger three times. He made a fist and rapped his knuckle once on the wooden desktop.

"I'm sorry, I can't help you."

He stood and opened the door and motioned through the doorway, "Thanks for coming in."

Something felt odd about the way he dismissed me, I didn't trust his feigned ignorance.

"Is there someone else in the department who—"

"No," he interrupted, "nobody here can help you."

He closed his office door and left me standing dumbfounded in the hallway. But I felt more than embarrassment; there was more to this mystery than he was letting on. I wondered how many other historians were keeping quiet too.

• • •

EVENTUALLY, ROBUST SEARCH ENGINES were developed to crawl the internet and catalog public websites. I would occasionally do a search for Delgado Pass, but the results always came back void. I discovered a new feature of these search engines which allowed you to set up a search alert. When new content was found matching a specified search term, it sent an email directly to you. This was a very appealing option—have the information pushed to me instead of having to endure the frustration of manual searches that never found anything.

I felt empowered by this wonderful tool. Perhaps it was the way to finally solve the mystery. Each day I'd eagerly check my email. But alas, the repeated lack of notifications meant no new information was found. I eventually stopped obsessively refreshing my browser and fell into wait mode.

But each day of hopeful waiting eventually added up to ten more years of total silence.

• • •

ONE EVENING AFTER WORK I was sitting in my car at a stoplight. I was trying to find a radio station that didn't have the same crappy music I grew up with—*Classic hits of the '70s, '80s, '90s, and today!* Pure crap. I turned it off. I was scrolling through email on my phone when I saw it—a notification from my long-forgotten search term alert. I wanted to read further but the car horns behind me became impatient—*get off your damn phone.*

When I got home I hurried to my computer and opened the email. Someone had published an obituary and the deceased was born in Delgado Pass. A small section of the webpage it had found was reproduced in the message:

> *Eleanor Brosseau-Young was born in 1940 in Delgado Pass, Arizona to François and Adrienne (Gaudin) Brosseau. Ellie is survived by ...*

I read the sentence again. After all these years of silence, the town had reemerged. My heart raced. I clicked the accompanying link and was taken to the obituary page of a funeral home. I read the listing:

> *Eleanor Brosseau-Young was born in 1940 in Denver, Colorado to François and Adrienne (Gaudin) Brosseau.*

Wait, Denver? That's not what my email said. There was no text of *Delgado Pass* anywhere in the obituary. I opened up another browser and did a search for the town but as always before, no results came back.

This was no mistake. Email alerts contain exactly what the search found—if it was in the email, it had been scraped from the site exactly as it appeared. Delgado Pass was intentionally listed as the birthplace but had been changed to Denver. The name of the town had, again, been erased from existence right before my eyes.

I read through the obituary and found that the visitation was two days later in a funeral home about thirty minutes from my house. I decided to do something completely out of my comfort zone; I was going to attend the visitation of a complete stranger.

I DUG OUT MY ILL-FITTING BLACK SUIT from the back of the closet and found the darkest tie I owned. My sweaty fingers struggled to remember how to tie a double Windsor knot. I finally left it loosely tied at the neck so as to not draw attention to the embarrassment of a knot.

I arrived at the funeral home late and pulled into the empty lot on the north side of the building. All other visitors seemed to be parked in the larger west lot outside the main entrance. My hands became clammy as I thought about what I would say if anyone approached me.

I'm a friend of the deceased.
But how would I explain the connection?
I'm a former coworker.
But where did she work, and when?
I'm friends with her son.
But he will likely be here and I don't know what he looks like.
I'm from the church.
That's probably the safest thing to say, *I'm from the church*—but considering my lack of knowledge about churches in the area, I figured it was best to just not speak with anyone.

I walked across the empty lot with nerves on edge and nausea building in my throat. It had been a long time since I was in high school, but this felt worse than the anticipation of my afternoon speech class presentation. I became dizzy and my vision was blurring. I took a deep breath and diverted my path to circle the west parking lot.

I knew there was nothing rational about my fear, nothing bad could come from stepping into the celebration of a stranger. But my emotions were roaring—I couldn't ignore the possibility that someone inside had known the girl on the swing.

I had never shared with anyone the fact that for years I had dreamt of her every night. Or that in my mind I could smell her lavender perfume. Or that I knew the softness of her sweater as I touched her back in the ice cream parlor. My most private and vulnerable thoughts seemed to be at stake.

I slowed as I approached the entry door. A man about my same age was leaning at ease against one of the giant Roman columns. He wore a topaz blue blazer over the top of a lemon yellow golf shirt. His khaki slacks barely touched the top of brown loafers. I kept my eyes low and tried to avoid eye contact.

"Who are *you*, man?" he asked as I was about to pass him.

"Sorry?"

"Who are you? I've never seen you before," he said as he cupped his hands around a cigarette to light it.

"I'm here for the visitation."

He drew in a deep breath of smoke and blew it upward as he looked sideways at me.

"That's not what I asked," he said as he flicked the cigarette with his thumb.

"I ... I'm a friend of the family's."

He looked me up and down, then looked at the filter of his cigarette. He took another deep inhale and said, "No you're not." His jacket sleeve slid to expose a barbed wire tattoo encircling his wrist.

"What do you mean ... why do you say that?"

"You're wearing black."

I looked down at my jacket sleeves and said, "Which is customary for visitations and funerals."

"Not this one," he said as he crossed one arm and tucked it under the other.

"And why's that?"

He leaned toward me and said, "If you *were* a friend of the family, which you're not, you would have heard that Ellie didn't want anything somber and black at her funeral. She wanted everyone to wear summertime colors to express their joy for her life."

He ran his open hand down the front of his torso like a game show host presenting a prize.

I rubbed my clammy fingers into my palms. Inside my jacket, sweat trickled from my armpit to my elbow.

The man with the topaz blazer brought his cigarette up to his mouth but stopped an inch away. He fixed his gaze on me with unblinking eyes. "So who are you really?"

I became unsettled by his sternness, I hadn't really planned an answer for this situation. The corner of his eye twitched once. He was laser-focused.

But before I could speak, he said, "I already know."

"What?" I said, startled.

"You're government—a pathetic G-man. I can spot you a mile away."

He pointed to a car where a man with dark glasses was speaking on a phone, "There's another one of you right there, watching me right now. Wave to your friend."

"I am *not* government," I exclaimed.

He pushed the cigarette toward my face and firmed up his voice, "Then who the hell are you?"

It was apparent that things were about to get ugly with Mr. Topaz Blazer.

"All right, all right!" I said as I lifted my palms in submission, "I don't know the family—you're right, yes."

His gaze remained fixed.

"I got an alert—a search alert—for Delgado Pass."

He raised an eyebrow.

I continued, "I've been looking for that town name for years and I got notified that a woman who had passed away was born there. I wanted to speak to her family."

He held his unblinking eyes on me, "So you're stalking a funeral, about the name of a town?"

"I saw it in an encyclopedia when I was a kid, but then it was just ... gone. Like it never existed. I think something bad happened—something *really* bad. I could never get it out of my head."

The man flicked the filter of his cigarette and said, "So what?"

"You see ... there was a picture of a girl, on a swing. Always thought she was so beautiful—always wondered what happened to her. I'm serious—that's the only reason I'm here. I can show you."

"If there ever *was* a town named Durango Path, and a disappearing girl on a swing has you stalking this funeral, you'd *really* need to show me that, man."

"I can—I have it in my car—right over there. I'll show you," I said with excitement.

He dropped his cigarette and stepped on it as we walked toward the north parking lot.

When he spotted my car, he said, "Nineteen fifty-seven Chevy Bel Air. Original condition Sierra Gold, unmodded ... impressive."

I responded, "There's no need to mess with perfection."

He caressed the waxed front fender as I unlocked the driver's side door and moved aside a folded gray sweatshirt. The pale blue D book from my youth was lying on the seat. I picked it up and handed it to him.

"Really?" he said in disbelief.

"Also nineteen fifty-seven, it's the only evidence I've ever found that the town and the girl even existed."

He asked, "What was that town again?"

"Delgado Pass ... Delgado ..." I said.

He flipped through the pages until he found it. He inspected the three photos with a slow nod.

"Well, there it is. Your funeral-disrupting town."

He held his gaze on the photo of the girl for an uncomfortably long time. His eyes began to tear up. He reached to place his fingertip next to her smile.

"I haven't seen this photo for a long time," he said with a slight nod, "Mom used to have it in a frame when I was growing up. Her little brother was so cute—but someone broke into our house and stole it. They broke in and stole only *one* thing, this photo from our fireplace mantle."

"Why would someone steal it? Wait—your fireplace mantle? That girl in the photo is your mother? Is she here?"

"Is she here? ..." he said behind a muted laugh, "It's her funeral, man."

I winced and turned toward the funeral home and back again. I rubbed my face with my palm and said, "I'm so sorry. What even happened ... to her, and the town?"

"They erased it off the map," he said as he tapped on the aerial photo, "she told me the story many times. About a year after this picnic photo, my grandfather got a new camera and he took Mom up onto the mountain to show her how to use it. Then they saw it."

"Saw what?"

"A blinding flash of light which faded into a slow-rising mushroom cloud. My grandfather was able to take a photo, but his camera was stolen before he developed the film."

"What happened, what exploded?"

"Don't know for sure."

He wiggled his finger at me and smiled, "You know what I think, man? I think it was a broken arrow—an accidental detonation they didn't want the public to know about."

"Broken arrow ... a nuke? Are you saying they accidentally blew up the town with a *nuke*?"

"That is exactly what I'm saying. Maybe not as big as *Little Boy*, but if it wasn't one of ours, we would have been at war, man. Within two days the government appropriated the whole area to make it a top-secret military zone. You've heard of Area 51? This was bigger—*way* bigger, the biggest coverup in American history.

"They erased all traces that it ever existed. They stopped all vehicles throughout the state, confiscated any driver's license with the town name. They destroyed every book that mentioned it. They removed all maps from every gas station—and I mean *every* gas station in the country—any that might show even the slightest dot or discoloration near Delgado Pass.

"And it's still going on. User searches are monitored in real-time. Agents are sent to estate sales and to scour antique shops looking for old books and maps. There's fewer things to find now, but every once in a while a book like this will show up."

He closed the book and handed it back to me, "You'd better keep this hidden. They will stop at nothing to get it."

I wrapped the book in my sweatshirt and opened the trunk. I lifted my jumper cables and placed the protected book underneath.

I said, "Every online search I've ever done returns nothing. So why did I briefly see Delgado Pass in the online obituary?"

"Aside from the cheerful attire, my mother also asked to publish the truth about where she was born and where she grew up. And where she wore her poodle skirt on a picnic with her family."

"Did they hack the site and change it to Denver?" I asked.

He nodded, "Immediately."

We began walking and as we reached the giant pillars framing the entry doors, he pulled out his cigarettes and lit another.

"Not many people know about what happened. And no one will believe you when you tell them. I've tried—believe me, I've tried. And if you've been searching online ... man, they already know about you," he said as he pointed to the man sitting in his car.

He stared at his cigarette and shook his head, "Go on in, I need a few moments. We'll chat later."

"Of course," I nodded and went inside.

The cermony was underway as I inched up to the archway of a large visitation room. The open casket was on the opposite end of the room. A woman stood at the podium sharing a memory of when she and Ellie had visited the arboretum light show and how it was such a wonderful night.

Several more guests took the podium and shared their own treasured memories. I stepped out of the archway and slowly paced the lobby while I read the memorial pamphlet. Consistent with the online obituary, it said she was born and raised in Denver and went on to attend Northwestern University. It was there she met her future husband David and they moved to Indianapolis where they raised their three children.

My head was down as I turned a corner into a hallway. An elderly woman stood wiping her tears and we startled each other.

"I'm so sorry, ma'am ... completely my fault," I said, embarrassed.

"No, it's my fault, I wasn't looking. It's just so sad, I can't believe she's gone."

"Yes, I know," I said with sympathy.

As she cleared her eyes, she said, "I'm sorry, I don't think we've met."

"Yes, hi, I'm from the church. It's nice to meet you."

We shared a brief awkward silence until I said, "How did you know Ellie?"

"I knew her since we were six years old, we lived on the same street."

"In Denver, or was it Delgado—" I paused with raised eyebrows.

"We grew up in a tiny town called Larkspur, tiny little thing."

"Did she move away as a teenager? To another state maybe?"

"Oh, no, we both lived in Larkspur until she went off to Chicago for college. But I never made it to college."

This version of Ellie's story didn't match what her son had told me outside.

"What ever happened to Ellie's little brother?" I quizzed her.

"Ellie didn't have a brother. Just an older sister named Louise, but she passed a while back."

Embarrassment swelled inside. I squinted and rolled the pamphlet into a tube.

I said, "I met Ellie's son once but I've forgotten what he looks like, could you point him out to me?"

"Of course," she said, and we entered the archway.

She leaned into me and whispered, "Right there, in the front row next to the little girl with the flower in her hair."

The man's face was hidden, but he was not wearing a lemon yellow golf shirt with a topaz blazer—it was black.

"Are you sure?" I whispered back.

"Of course. I'll introduce you after the ceremony."

It was then I realized that nearly everyone was wearing black. I left Ellie's friend at the archway and hurried outside.

Mr. Topaz Blazer was not there. I stepped out into the parking lot but couldn't spot him anywhere. I turned to where the government car was parked but it was gone.

"Crap," I said as I kicked the cigarette butt he had dropped.

No detail of his story matched this woman's obituary. There was no way the woman lying in that coffin was my girl on the swing. And I would have placed wages that nobody inside would have even heard of Delgado Pass.

I ran toward my car and opened the trunk. My sweatshirt was thrown aside and the book was gone.

"Dammit!" I yelled.

It's plausible everything Topaz Blazer said about the government was true. I think they knew I had been searching for Delgado Pass for a long time, and they lured me in with the altered obituary. But he failed to mention one important detail— that he was also one of them. I raised my palm to rub my eyes, then slapped my forehead. *You idiot!* They were expecting me to show up and I literally just placed the book into their hands.

I sat in my car for a long time that day. I was so angry for being swindled. I was so saddened that the last remaining trace of my favorite town was gone. And my auburn angel on the swing—I had looked at her photo thousands of times, but I'd never get just once more. I knew I'd lose the feel of her soft sweater. I knew the calm of her lavender perfume would fade from my memory.

• • •

CHEMOTHERAPY TREATMENTS have been increasingly horrendous. I can barely do anything but sit in my recliner and look at my bookcase. I have neither the energy nor focus to read the books anymore. I often think of Dad and how he influenced my love of reading and learning. I laugh at how my recliner is positioned just as his was; an optimum location for consuming our books.

I occasionally drift out of consciousness and arrive in Delgado Pass. I'm stepping off the train car and I see my auburn-haired girl. She walks over to me and grabs my hand.

I've been waiting for you.

I feel my 12-year-old cheeks blush at her words. We go to the ice cream parlor and share a malted milkshake while birds sing in the sunshine. It's heaven and it's wonderful.

As I drift back and open my eyes, a man is standing in front of my recliner. His gray golf shirt hugs a protruding belly and a satchel is slung across his shoulder. He raises a friendly hand and his wrist is encircled with a tattoo of barbed wire. His face confuses me at first but I finally make out that this man is an aged Topaz Blazer.

In my loudest painful whisper, I say, "You son of a bitch."

He kneels down in front of me and places his hand on my knee.

"I'm sorry. I had to do it. The government led you to that funeral home and was going to hurt you to get the book. I took them off your trail. That's what I do."

After a long pause, I whisper, "Who are you?"

"I was honest about what happened to the town. And that the girl on the swing was my mother. I only lied that you were at her funeral. Everything the government was watching … we were watching too. A small group of us dedicated our lives to preserving the existence of Delgado Pass. And you helped us. But I truly am sorry."

Topaz Blazer opens the satchel and slowly removes something that I recognize—my 1957 World Book encyclopedia D book. He extends it out but I'm too weak to raise my hand. He nods and nestles his fingertip into the front pages. He eases the leather covers apart and turns the book toward me. He's opened it right to the Delgado Pass entry.

There they are again, the happy family enjoying a picnic near a blossoming magnolia tree. They are still laughing at the world's corniest joke.

And there she is. Her smile is bright and that perfect auburn hair is pulled back into a ponytail. Her toes are still pointed inside the saddle shoes. And she's still sitting on the swing.

My eyes smile but I don't have enough energy to reach for the book.

I'm drifting away …

THE BLACK STEAM ENGINE BILLOWS its final cloud as it pulls to a stop at the Delgado Pass station. My nerves are calm as I step off the passenger car and into the sunshine. My ears fill with the songs of birds professing love for each other. Then my angel slowly ascends the steps to the platform, her auburn ponytail sways to a stop as the sunlight enhances her glow. She holds her eyes down for a beautiful moment, then lifts them to meet mine.

All other passengers blur away into the brightness. It's only her and I. Her smile widens and plumps out her beautiful cheeks into dimples. She waves. I wave back. She approaches and the beautiful birdsongs fade into silence.

I've been waiting for you.

My 12-year-old cheeks blush, and with a smile, we both turn toward the ice cream parlor. I reach to hold her hand as she reaches for mine. We walk, but it's more like floating through a warm dreamscape—it's what happiness was always supposed to feel like. The sun becomes brighter, wrapping me in peaceful calm and assurance.

For a lifetime I've held on to hope. But now, I hold an angel. And my auburn angel holds me.

THE H BUS

G ARRISON FLOWERS STOOD at the intersection of two bone-dry gravel roads, somewhere far out in the barren countryside it seemed. And he couldn't remember how he got there. The sun was high and blinding, perhaps it was noon, maybe late afternoon, but Flowers had no sense of time.

The air was hot—so very hot. Flowers' sweat increased under his expensive necktie and pressed wool suit. His forehead perspiration dripped and ran down his temple across his cheek. He reached into his jacket pocket for a handkerchief, but it wasn't there.

"Where is that damn ..." he said, searching his remaining pockets. He wiped his brow with his sleeve but the sweat kept dripping.

Far down the road to his left, a cloud of gravel dust swirled, growing and creeping closer. Flowers tried to determine what was inside but he could only hear a low sputtering grumble encased in all that dust. Dips in the road caused a loud banging of old metal against old metal. This was some large machine.

As the cloud approached, a clutch engaged and gears ground together, resisting change as old gears are wont to do. Suddenly, worn-out brake pads squealed, driving a painful shrieking spike right through Flowers's head.

As the cloud slowed to a stop, the round faded green face of an old rust-speckled bus emerged. A weathered decal boasted its owner as the NYC Transit. The banner in the window declared that it was *Not In Service*, but every passenger window revealed a sweaty, emotionless face staring straight ahead.

Flowers squinted and coughed from the dust. With small steps, he turned full circle looking in every direction trying to figure out what a New York City Transit bus, many decades old, was doing in the middle of wherever-this-is.

The doors opened to reveal the driver, an elderly black man in a gray long-sleeve NYC Transit shirt, sharply sporting a black bowtie. The front of his shirt clung to his portly belly. The driver was already wearing a giant smile as he grabbed his cap by the brim and gave it a little tip.

"Good day, sir, I'm suspectin' you need a ride!" he said with enthusiasm.

Flowers scrunched his face and squinted from the sun.

"Where are you going?"

"Well, I'm headed the same way you are," the driver said as he pointed through the front windshield.

Flowers scanned the passengers in the windows, but none returned even a glance.

"You got any room?"

"Oh, my! I've always got room for one more. Come on in, sir!" the driver said with joy.

Flowers placed a foot onto the first step and paused. He lifted his hand to shade his eyes and turned to look left down the road from which the bus approached. The dusty gravel seemed oddly straight and ran all the way to touch the horizon. And the other way, again nothing but an endless, straight gravel road. Each direction of this road was a mirror image of the other.

He stepped onto the bus.

"Please, sit right here," the driver said as he waved his hand to the seat directly behind him.

Flowers looked at the front seat with the single empty pad, then skimmed over the rest of the bus. This was the only available spot, so he sat.

The driver closed the door and cheerfully nodded his head, "Welcome aboard, Mr. Flowers. Next stop, barbecue!"

Flowers responded, "Hey—how do you know me?"

"Well, I wouldn't be much of a host if I didn't know who my guests were," the driver said with pride.

"You know everybody on this bus? I don't think so."

"Oh, yes sir, I sure do. Who would you like to meet?"

Flowers glanced around and saw an assortment of shady characters, all looking at him with the worn, weary dread of a long bus ride.

"No, that's okay," he said and turned back to the driver, "I'm more interested in that barbecue."

The driver laughed and nodded with great approval as he slapped the steering wheel, "Now that's what I like to hear!"

He forced the grinding gears where they did not want to go and set the bus in motion.

The interior of the bus was uncomfortably hot. Flowers noticed that none of the windows could be opened, they were a single pane of glass.

"What a weird old bus," Flowers muttered under his breath.

Unnoticed by Flowers, the driver had been watching him in his mirror.

AFTER A WHILE OF DRIVING through the dry, featureless countryside—Flowers was uncertain how long it had been—he said to the driver, "You look familiar, have we met before?"

"Most certainly yes!" he said, "I was hoping you'd remember me, oh yes! I used to drive your route when you lived in New York City—you would take the H bus home at night. I think you had just started college … if I remember rightly."

Flowers absorbed the driver's words as he tried to remember that time from so many years ago.

The driver continued, "You said once that I made you feel comfortable, seein' how you were new to the city and all."

The driver lightly tapped himself on the chest, directly over his heart, and smiled from the memory.

"I do—I do remember," stated Flowers, "But how can you be here? Am I dreaming all of this?"

"Oh, no. No sir, this is not a dream. You were lost and in need of a comforting face, so here I am to be driving you."

Flowers was still confused but didn't want to risk insulting the driver, so he responded, "Thank you, I do remember being comfortable with you. It's good to see you again."

The driver slapped the steering wheel again and said, "Now that's what I like to hear! Welcome aboard, oh yes—welcome aboard!"

AFTER A LONGER WHILE, OR MAYBE it was shorter—Flowers couldn't decide—the driver slowed to pull onto the shoulder of that perfectly straight road. He squealed the brakes to a stop in front of a roadside barbecue stand.

A large cloud of gravel dust engulfed the bus as the driver mumbled to himself, "Here we is, here we is!"

As the cloud cleared, Flowers noticed that there were no other vehicles or people anywhere around.

He asked the driver, "Are you sure they're open?"

The driver laughed as he opened the door, "They're always open for me, oh yes."

Flowers had been hungry all day, and the heat inside the bus was intense, so he was relieved at the thought of some fresh air and tasty barbecue. As he stood, the driver grabbed his shoulder and pushed him back down into the seat.

"Oh no, you can't leave the bus. This stop is only for me."

Flowers looked up at the driver, as confused as he had been

all day, "We can't leave the bus, why not?"

"That would be a bit much, now wouldn't it Mr. Flowers?" the driver said sternly before he stepped out onto the gravel.

He opened his arms wide and shouted toward the large smoker grill, "I'm here, hopes you got enough to satisfy me!"

Flowers watched in disbelief as the driver cackled and shuffled his feet in a little dance. Flowers turned around to engage the other passengers, but their eyes were fixed on him with uninterested, unblinking stares. One cocky-looking girl with green hair raised a single eyebrow. Flowers took a deep swallow—which, at this point, was difficult due to his parched throat—and turned to face forward.

A SHORT WHILE LATER, OR MAYBE it was a long time—it was hard for Flowers to tell—the driver came back. Rubbing his big belly, he announced, "All right, all fueled up, let's get on with it!"

Again he forced the grinding gears where they did not want to go and started driving. He waved goodbye toward the smoker grill, but Flowers couldn't see anyone who might wave back. In fact, he hadn't seen anyone else outside the whole time they were parked, however long that was.

As they picked up speed, Flowers spoke in a weakened voice, "Hey, which way are we headed, because—man is it getting hot in here."

The driver pointed through the windshield and said, "South, of course." He winked at the green-haired girl. She sneered back.

Flowers shifted in his seat, doubting there was any padding between him and the seat's metal frame. He tried to wipe his forehead again but could not remove any sweat. His chest had been hurting since he stepped on the bus, but now he could feel his pulse throbbing inside his shirt collar.

He said in an increasingly dry rasp, "Something isn't kosher here—why are we riding on this miserable bus, with you as my driver—looking exactly like you did fifty years ago—no idea where we're going—and all these dead-faced people who don't seem to have anything to say. I don't get it."

The driver pursed his lips and said in a calm tone, "You're right, this must seem very odd."

He paused to collect his thoughts, then continued, "For one thing, I don't look like this to everyone, only you. This is the comforting face I wear just for you, the one you needed. The woman behind you, to her I look like her grandmother—the nice one. The guy behind her, I look like his old boss—the one he had a crush on."

The driver winked at Flowers, "That's why he keeps staring at me like that."

Flowers shook his head and kneaded his suddenly painful arm, "What the hell are you talking about?"

The driver responded sternly, "Now, now, Mr. Flowers! Language—let's not go dropping the H-word on this bus, are we clear?"

Flowers tried as hard as he could to remember how he ended up at that intersection of those perfectly straight gravel roads, just before the bus came along. He struggled, but his only clear memory was having just been in the corporate boardroom with his lawyers. They were discussing the details of their hostile takeover of a pesky competitor. This next deal was going to be big, and all those thousands of redundant laborers would be cut and the profits would skyrocket.

Flowers couldn't connect these scenarios—somehow going from his boardroom to a remote wasteland, riding this hot-as-Hell bus. He massaged his painful shoulder as the driver watched him in the mirror.

"I died," Flowers tried to say to himself, but his voice was wispy from dehydration, "I must have died ... my heart."

He winced in pain as he tried to swallow.

The driver moved his eyes off the mirror and back to the road ahead. He spoke with calm patience, "Now, now, Mr. Flowers, that's about all you're going to be able to say from now on. It's a long trip so I suggest you settle in."

Fear swelled inside Flowers. He turned to the cocky green-haired girl, his face full of panic. But she had no sympathy for him, she just rolled her eyes in silent boredom.

AFTER A SHORT WHILE, OR MAYBE it was a long while—Flowers couldn't tell—the driver turned to him and said, "Looks like we got us a new passenger, would you mind movin' back one seat, Mr. Flowers? Thank you kindly."

Flowers stood and turned around. Everyone sitting behind him was now shifted one seat further back. Flowers took his new seat; exhausted, sweaty, and emotionless.

The brakes squealed a painful shriek and the bus came to a stop at the same intersection of those two perfectly straight gravel roads. It was still noon, or maybe late afternoon.

A young woman in a bright yellow summer dress was waiting, staring at the bus, immobilized from confusion.

The driver opened the door and declared with an enthusiastic tip of his hat, "Good day, ma'am, I'm suspectin' you need a ride!"

"Where are you going?" she asked.

"Well, I'm headed the same way you are," he said as he pointed through the front windshield, "Oh, yes, we're all headed the same way."

SAVAGES

———————

I HAD TRAVELED SINCE THE MORNING, toward the river's end. Grandfather rarely sent me in that direction but today he was expecting important visitors and instructed me to be mindful of his standing. Usually he would send me into the hills for my explorations. Sometimes I would head toward the woods or the river's beginning. I never actually found the river's beginning, but I have learned a great many things about nature and her spirits in all directions.

I NEVER KNEW MY FATHER. Grandfather explained how the nature spirits channeled through Father with great strength, but he was reluctant to use his power. He was killed by the savages as they tormented him to become things that he would not. They killed him and threw him in the river and let his blood drain and flow toward river's end. That is what they do.

Grandfather and I ended up alone, the last members of our family and the last to make this beautiful valley our home. He spoke of a time when our communities flourished and the savages did not exist. I am eighteen winters old, but I do not think even Grandfather knew his own age. His long hair was winter white, where it was once black as the night sky, just like mine, he had told me.

His wisdom was vast and I learned much from him. He had taught me to become one with the spirits of nature. He taught me to learn from everything I see and every creature I meet.

And he had taught me about the savages and how they want to take all of nature and her spirits from us.

Grandfather said I should travel on the air spirits, like he did when he was younger, to make the most distance in my travels. He was right, and sometimes I would. But mostly I liked to travel as a leopard so that I could move fast if I needed to, but also slow and quiet if I wished. I liked to feel the earth under each step. I could jump high and crouch low, but I just liked how it felt to glide when running. And I felt patience as a leopard.

I HAD BEEN WATCHING THE TREE spirits perform a dance with the wind spirits when I smelled it, the faint scent of blood. It came from the river so I approached and took a drink. I tasted blood. I leaped toward the middle of the river and became a fish, letting the water flow around me and flow through my gills.

In his teachings of nature, Grandfather made sure I knew the importance of the spirits and all creatures, so I was familiar with blood. This was my Grandfather's blood.

I became an eagle and flew as straight as I could and as fast as I could. As I approached our home from high above, I spotted four savages sitting in a circle smoking their pipes. They were joyful and relaxed.

I diverted toward the river and saw Grandfather lying face down in the river rocks, his white hair flowing toward river's end. I landed on my feet as a man and pulled him out of the water. All of the nature spirits had left his body and he was lifeless.

He had been preparing me for many things and many adventures, but I was not prepared for his death.

I became a leopard and sprinted back to our home. As I approached in silence, the savages spoke in their ugly language and laughed with each other and seemed pleased about Grandfather.

Their skin was as pale as Grandfather had once described. He had told me the story of how the spirits refused to inhabit savages and how the spirits had drained all healthy color from their skin. Since savages were filled with evil and had allowed their evil to fade all goodness from their souls, they would forever wear pale skin as punishment.

The spirits seemed to unleash me as I filled with anger. I pounced on one of the savages and tore off most of his neck. As I threw him aside, I landed on my feet as a man and spread my arms wide in warning. I had never felt this anger, the beautiful calm had left me.

The savages circled me as they raised their firearms. One of them flinched a finger to fire a shot and I became a pebble and dropped to the ground. His bullet felled one of the other savages.

The remaining two yelled with panic at each other and lowered their firearms. One of them nudged me with his foot, and I struggled not to respond, I remained a pebble. He nudged me with his finger, then picked me up. He laughed in relief and held me above his head, mocking how small and unthreatening I had become. As he held me high, I could not contain myself and became a chunk of mountain and crushed his body.

As the last savage stood frozen in disbelief, I became a blueberry and rolled toward his feet. Fear kept him frozen. In time, relief spread across his face as he developed a plan. As quickly as he could, he picked me up and placed me in his mouth and bit down.

My thoughts were with Grandfather as I first touched the tongue of the savage. Grandfather had taught me many things about nature and her spirits, and about the small and clever creatures that survive in the harshest conditions. But he also taught me about the large and passive animals, and how they do not let the small clever creatures bother them, and how they survive harsh conditions as well.

So I became an ox. It did not fare well for the savage, as an ox had just formed inside of his mouth.

NOW AS I SIT HERE WATCHING THE SUN spirits fade off to rest, I wonder if Grandfather sent me toward the river's end on purpose. I wonder if he was preparing to die.

I wonder if he knew all along the savages would take his life, and that he would restrain himself from fighting back. I wonder if he did not want me here to prevent it. I wonder if he knew I would smell his spirit in the river, long after it had left his body.

I miss Grandfather, but I know that he lives on in the spirits of nature, that he lives on within all creatures, and that he lives on within me, with great strength. And I know that he wants me to keep our home and our beautiful valley safe, to keep it from the savages, and to keep the nature spirits alive.

But unlike my father, I am not reluctant to use my power.

I am the last member of my family, but I am strong and one with the spirits of nature. They have always comforted me, shaped my thoughts, filled my lungs, pulsed in my veins. And I know they will embrace what is to come, what I must do.

I become an eagle and fly toward the river's end, ready to travel farther than I have ever before. I always listened to Grandfather's wisdom. In life, and now in death.

Grandfather recently told me that savages like to make their villages along rivers, places much too dangerous for me to explore. His words spoke of safety and avoidance. But his true teachings are now clear—he taught me how to be strong, he taught me how to find savages, and he taught me how to hunger for revenge.

GUSTAVO'S CHAIR

GUSTAVO AWOKE NEARLY AN HOUR before sunrise, having slept the night in his trusty, tufted, wingback leather chair. Gustavo hadn't felt this refreshed for quite a while, probably since the day he opened his last shop. He loved his other shop, but it was time to move on, away from that city, time to meet new faces and forget about the old.

A handsome, yet modest Italian man, Gustavo's black hair and smooth skin belied him as just a boy, barely out of school, it would seem. But inside that youthful skin, he was an old soul and quite an old-world expert leatherworker. He studied under the best master craftsman in Italy when he was much younger, and now his passion and experience have made him one of the best craftsmen in the new country.

The day prior, in preparation for the grand opening of the new shop, Gustavo reupholstered his comfortable old chair. Upon relocating his business to this new and exciting city, Gustavo decided his chair needed a makeover, a chance to look young again so that they could share in outward youth together. The leather had been thinning and showing age with worn seams and faded color, but the frame was steadfast and solid.

When finished, he placed the chair next to his workbench as he had in the previous shop—out of reach of visiting customers, but close enough not to be forgotten that it has long been part of Gustavo's lineage. This is where he slept the night.

Gustavo's new shop thrived during the growing industrialization period. His proficiency in all things leather meant he rarely turned away business. Shoes were the most consistent request—for both repairs and new, but he also worked with purses, wallets, and hats. The city's use of horse-mounted police had been dwindling for some time, so requests for saddle repair were not as prominent as they had been in their heyday. Gustavo despised waste and would craft playful keychains out of unused scraps of leather, a special gift handed out to well-behaved children.

GUSTAVO TREATED ALL PEOPLE well. He was always friendly and personable even if his customers were foul and deserved none of his good tidings. One cold autumn day, two teenage boys came into the shop and giggled with nervous energy as they browsed over miscellaneous leather masterworks. Gustavo generally had trust in his shop guests, but these two reeked of trouble.

Flittering about the shop, the kids showed no interest in anything particular, picking things up and misplacing them back to random spots. Prior to these urchins arriving, Gustavo had been deep in focus on a project at his bench, but now had turned on his stool to watch them more closely.

"Can I help you find something?" Gustavo asked in his smokey Tuscan accent.

"We're fine, go back to work old man," the tall one said.

Gustavo wasn't offended by the insult, he thought he looked quite young for his age. He laughed and spread his arm out wide to rest on the bench. Then laughed louder.

"Something funny?" the tall kid said in defiance.

"You are disrupting my displays, could you show a little respect for my work, please?" Gustavo said with calm.

The kids looked at each other and turned toward Gustavo. The short one wore a smirk and nodded as if someone had just offered him a candy apple. The tall one squinted and approached Gustavo with his head tilted in spite.

"Maybe you should show *us* a little respect," the tall one said, "we're the reason you even have a business."

"I remember all of my customers, and you certainly are not the reason I have good business."

The tall one became irritated, "Do you know who I am? I own this neighborhood. I could spread the word about this terrible shop and you'd never have a customer again."

"I beg to differ," Gustavo said after a slow blink.

The tall one turned and thrust himself down into Gustavo's chair. Gustavo smiled and nodded at the bravado.

The tall one reached into his breast pocket and pulled out a small hunting knife, widening his defiant smile. He pointed the knife at Gustavo and began, "Maybe ..."

Gustavo didn't flinch.

The kid flipped the knife in his palm to point the blade downward.

"... I can teach you," he said as he lowered the blade to the arm of the chair.

"to respect ..."

When Gustavo had spread his arm out on his bench, he positioned his hand next to his largest kiridashi knife. He snatched it up, jumped off his stool, and in one smooth motion, pulled the kid's hair back to press the knife to his throat.

"Police chief O'Shaughnessy is a customer of mine and if he came in here and saw you bloody and dead in my chair with that pathetic knife in your hand, he'd probably thank me for cleaning up his city."

The kid's eyes widened, he pulled the knife away from the chair and returned it to his jacket.

Gustavo applied more pressure to the kid's throat.

"Get out of my chair."

The kid cautiously lifted himself out of the chair and backed toward the door.

"You're crazy, old man! And your stupid chair is about as comfortable as a sack of bricks," he said before rushing out the door.

Gustavo watched the two scuttle down the sidewalk, then said to himself, "That's because it doesn't like you."

• • •

YEARS LATER, GUSTAVO WELCOMED a customer into his shop— an elderly woman, frail and sad. Gustavo was a natural at recognizing a soul in need, and he noticed the woman's distant gaze— as if happiness had been slowly draining through her shallow breath.

Gustavo greeted her with pleasantries, as was his nature, and was compassionate as he listened when she confessed her concerns about the upcoming weekend. She was to visit her daughter in the countryside to celebrate her grandson's birthday. But she hadn't been feeling well and was having a dark notion about her health and longevity.

The woman had come to Gustavo to fix a broken strap on her purse, a very simple procedure requiring only one or two minutes, but he told her he would need forty if she didn't mind waiting. He insisted she sit in his chair while he worked, a guest in his comfortable, most prized possession. She refused at first, but he insisted until she finally complied.

A few short moments after settling into the chair, the woman fell asleep. Gustavo knew what she needed most was a rest, and he smiled with contentment as she drifted away. He fixed the purse with no effort and retrieved one of his playful keychains from a basket under the register and slipped it into her purse, a free gift for her grandson.

Gustavo took note of when the woman had fallen asleep and continued about his shop working on other projects. At exactly twenty-four minutes into her rest, Gustavo woke the woman. He told her he was finished, that the fix was quicker than he thought and was guaranteed to last the lifetime of the purse. The woman was slightly embarrassed by nodding off and heartily apologized to Gustavo, but he dismissed all apologies.

As the fog cleared from her head, the woman wore a different expression than when she had entered the shop. Her face was full of resolve and hope as she took a deep, slow breath. She said she was no longer feeling ill and her heart was relaxed and comfortable. Gustavo expressed his happiness for her and insisted she simply needed his pleasant company and therapeutic words, and for her lungs to breathe the warm, wonderful aroma of tanned leather. She thanked him as he declined her payment, and she stepped out of the shop a refreshed woman.

Gustavo knew it wasn't his words or pleasant company or the aroma of the leather shop that lifted her health. He knew it was the chair.

· · ·

DECADES PASSED AND MANY THINGS changed in the city, but Gustavo's shop wasn't one of them. He had wisely chosen a location, so many years ago, near enough to the bustle of businessmen and their money, but far enough away from the greedy deals they sowed to enrich themselves. From those transactions, whole blocks of established neighborhoods and shops—both gritty and robust—had been wiped clean to erect towers of sterile glass and steel. But Gustavo's shop remained throughout.

GUSTAVO WAS NO LONGER THE YOUNG handsome man he once had been, the black of his hair had faded to gray long ago. His skin was thin and his wrinkles pronounced. His back was hunched and his fingers hurt to bend. The time had come, Gustavo decided, to close the shop. He had been thinking about this for some time and he always had good sense and faith about initiating change, and what his future would bring.

Gustavo spent the next week saying his goodbyes as he informed his loyal customers and friends of his plans. They threw Gustavo a small party in his shop and laughter resounded and tears fell. They all commented on Gustavo's wonderful chair and took turns sitting in it one last time. The leather was showing its age and the seams were again worn and faded as they had been so many years before.

"Gustavo," a woman inquired, "what will become of your leather goods and your antique tools? Are you selling them?"

"No, no ... I have secured a new home for my tools and surplus supplies. They will be put to good use once again."

"But what about your chair—you will give that away too? I would love to have it in my home if it is not part of your retirement plans."

"Oh, heavens no! My chair goes with me to my new home. I will look at it every day and think of all of you and the many, many folks over the years who have become my friends and enjoyed rejuvenation from my chair's comfort."

GUSTAVO MOVED WESTWARD AND SETTLED into a young and budding city. Unbeknownst to the friends and patrons he left behind, Gustavo opened a new shop therein. He loved his previous shop, but it was time to move on, away from that city, time to meet new faces and forget about the old.

The day prior to the grand opening of his new shop, Gustavo reupholstered his faithful old chair as he had done before. Then as the evening slowed to conclusion, Gustavo did something he only permitted himself once every sixty years, or so—he sat in his chair to sleep for the night.

• • •

FIVE CENTURIES AGO, LIGHTNING from a stormless sky felled a mighty oak in the Italian countryside, and an elderly craftsman ordained the wood to become the skeleton of a beautiful chair. The craftsman was a master leatherworker and he took special care in giving his chair an outward presentation of utmost beauty. Upon completion of his newly birthed chair and after the evening darkness set in, the aged craftsman, Gustavo, sat to rest.

The next morning when he awoke an hour before sunrise, Gustavo found himself wearing the body he had known as a much younger man. The appreciative chair, which had been given such a beautiful facade to wear, had repaid its creator with matching reciprocation. Gustavo was once again a handsome and young man full of robust energy. His back was straight and strong, his hair had returned to thick black follicles, and his skin was as smooth as when he was just a boy.

Fearing dishonest deeds if the newfound magic of his chair was discovered, Gustavo left his village and resumed his craft in a faraway town. He thrived for another lifetime and when he sensed his health failing in old age, Gustavo and his chair again made the transition to youth to start anew.

ONE DAY, PERHAPS, GUSTAVO will no longer care what the world will become. He will no longer cherish the future friendships he will form. He will tire of the smell and texture and suppleness of the leather in his fingers. One day he will surrender to Father Time.

But until that day, Gustavo will keep giving his chair new life, and his chair will return him the compliment.

THREE TWELVE

——————

FIVE CITY BLOCKS OF DIRTY brownstones lined the route home from Devin's school. The low afternoon sun bled shadows into recessed windows, defining sad, sullen faces within the cut stone facades. Devin studied the character of each as he passed. He was struck by the loneliness expressed by the shadows, which were only slightly darker than his own skin.

Devin stood at the end of the block, his eyes locked on the last of the despondent faces. It looked at Devin with worry. It seemed to know that Devin lived just past the intersection and it worried for his safety. But Devin knew he was safe; he knew he was protected.

With a pinch on his jacket sleeve, Devin's mother pulled him into motion as the stoplight changed to green.

"Come on, baby," Lily said.

Her voice was weary, but it only hinted at her deeper fatigue—she was tired from the sudden onset of cool weather, tired from the recent move into this neighborhood, and tired from raising her newly-teenage son on her own.

Devin's keen intelligence raced beneath a silent exterior. But his attention often wandered to unimportant distractions.

His focus could be vaporous, flowing in and out of thought, drifting and ambling. Or it could be immutable like the brownstones themselves, zeroing in on compelling patterns that others found mundane.

Devin pointed to a window on the third floor of the approaching apartment building. Lily didn't respond, wearily pretending not to notice. But as Devin continued walking with his arm outstretched and stiff, she relented and stopped with a firm pull on his backpack.

"What, Devin?" she begged, "What?"

Her eyes followed his finger up to the building, landing on a window identical to every other.

"Yes, I know. That's our apartment."

Devin opened his palm and waved to the window.

Lily sighed and said, "I'm happy that you're happy to be home."

She grabbed his backpack and tugged him toward the building as she resumed her impatient pace.

"I'm ready for Spaghetti Friday," she said, "You ready? Ready-spaghetti?"

Devin threw a last-second glance up to the window as they entered the building.

STEPPING OFF THE ELEVATOR, Lily and Devin entered the dim, pungent hallway. They passed through a gauntlet of ethnic world cooking, through an invisible wall of curry fumes and spicy peppers. Their apartment, 313, waited at the end of the hallway, the farthest from the elevator. As a corner unit, it was appealing to Lily for having fewer neighbors and less noise. But with such appeal, she had wondered why this highly desirable unit was still available to rent when she had been looking.

Devin studied the brass numbers tacked to their apartment door as Lily dug for her keys. The finish on the three metal pieces was inconsistent; the first '3' and '1' were tarnished and opaque, while the last '3' had a golden shine. He turned to the door across the hallway—number 311—its digits were all consistently aged.

Lily twisted her key and the deadbolt unlatched with a firm thunk. She pushed the door open and peeled Devin's backpack from his shoulders as they entered.

"Any homework?" Lily asked.

"Done."

"Figured. Any big plans for the weekend?"

Devin pulled his arms out of his jacket, leaving the sleeves inside out. He dropped it to the floor, missing Lily's outstretched hand. Without saying a word, he shuffled into his bedroom.

Lily, with her hand still waiting, looked down and sighed.

"I got it," she said.

• • •

STIFF SPAGHETTI STRANDS PROTRUDED from an old stainless steel pot of boiling water. Lily flattened the empty box and dropped it into the trash bin. The submerged pasta softened and Lily pressed with a wooden spoon to force the dry ends under water. She opened an upper cabinet door and scanned the shelves.

"I know I just got one," she mumbled.

She craned her neck for a better view of the highest shelf.

"Wouldn't be up there."

Confused, she called out, "Devin, have you seen the spaghetti sauce?"

She closed the cabinet and walked to Devin's room. He sat at a small desk, fully engaged in reading 'Electronics Recipes', a book thicker than any of his school textbooks. A draftsman's lamp spread its warm glow across his desk.

Lily leaned on the doorframe and repeated, "Baby, have you seen the spaghetti sauce?"

Devin lifted his eyes to her.

The creak of a kitchen cabinet door caught Lily's attention.

She leaned sideways to peer back into the kitchen while Devin's eyes remained fixed on her.

"What in the world?"

Devin resumed reading as Lily took hesitant steps toward the kitchen. She found the bottom cabinet door wide open, exposing pots and pans. Leaning in with cautious curiosity, she placed her palm on the countertop, which stung her skin with an ice-cold jolt.

"Holy—" she exclaimed as she pulled away and instinctively wiped her hand on her hip.

After inspecting her fingers in disbelief, she reached again for the countertop. One tiny tap of her fingertip revealed the surface to be the normal room temperature. Resting her hand flat again, she found nothing unusual.

"I am *too* tired," she said with a shake of her head.

From the corner of her eye, she noticed the jar of sauce resting in the middle of the countertop.

"Right in front of me the whole time," she mumbled.

"Devin," she announced over her shoulder, "wash up for dinner."

• • •

LILY CUT HER SPAGHETTI INTO SMALL bites with a fork before raising a scoop to her mouth. She held her eyes on Devin while her fork hung in midair.

"How was school today?"

"Fine," Devin said.

Lily brought the pasta to her mouth and chewed.

Pointing her fork tines at Devin, she mumbled through her full mouth, "Anybody pick on you today?"

Devin spun his fork in the spaghetti and lifted a large twirl to his mouth. He slurped the full bolus through his lips.

Lily set her fork down and planted her elbows. She interlaced her fingers in front of her mouth and said, "Who picked on you?"

Devin remained silent as he chewed and moved his eyes to the kitchen. He thought he had seen the wooden spoon shift inside the pot.

"Devin! Who picked on you?" Lily demanded.

Startled, Devin looked back at Lily. She clenched her mouth and raised her eyebrows.

"They're stupid," Devin said.

Lily slouched in her chair and rubbed her eyebrows, "God, I hate this school already."

Leaning forward, she reached her hand across the table to grab Devin's hand, but he ignored her.

"I am so sorry, baby. I know they are. I wish I could fix it—I wish I could fix all of it."

She thumped the tabletop with a closed fist, and immediately the bottom cabinet door popped open again, moving with a slow creak.

"What ..." Lily began.

She stood and crept toward the kitchen.

"... is going on?"

Hesitant to touch the countertop, she held her palm just off the surface.

"Don't be cold, don't be cold," she whispered to herself.

She lowered her fingertips to the surface and found it as warm as the room.

"Thank God. This is so crazy."

As she leaned to inspect the lower cabinet, a freezing jolt shot from the countertop through her supporting hand.

"Oh!" she screamed and jumped back.

Lily motioned to Devin, "Baby, could you come over here?"

Devin stood, approached Lily, and stopped at her side.

"Could you touch that counter? Right there?"

Devin glanced into the lower cabinet with a hint of a smile. He didn't understand her urgency.

"Right there, right there. Touch it," she said.

Devin rested his hand on the countertop and looked up at Lily. He held it for a moment then walked back to the dining table.

"Nothing?" Lily asked.

Devin sat.

"You didn't feel nothing?"

She turned and touched the countertop to find it warm again. "I'm not having this," she said.

• • •

LILY STRAIGHTENED HERSELF ON THE COUCH and set a magazine down. She squared her feet on the floor. Reaching for her phone, she bumped an emptied wine glass with her fingernail. The ping carried through the air and landed in Devin's ears. He looked up from his book and peered through the doorway. *Who was she calling?*

"Hey, it's me," Lily said into the phone.

"Could you stop by tomorrow? I got a kitchen cabinet having some problems, the door won't stay shut.

"I'd appreciate that," she said.

"Probably just hot dogs.

"Yes, you can. Maybe you could pick up a tomato or two on your way? That might earn you a second dog.

"Thanks," Lily said before setting the phone down.

Lily noticed Devin standing in his doorway, eavesdropping on her call.

"Hey baby, Leo's gonna stop by tomorrow."

"Why?"

"To fix that cabinet. He's good with that stuff."

"He doesn't need to."

"What do you mean? It keeps swinging open."

"It's not broken."

Devin turned and disappeared into his room.

Lily shook her head and sighed and pulled a throw pillow tightly to her chest.

• • •

A KNOCK CAME FROM THE FRONT door as Lily opened a pack of hot dogs.

"Devin, could you get that?" she called out.

She heard no response.

"Devin?"

Lily groaned and headed toward the door.

As she approached Devin's room, she noticed many circuitry components spread across his desk. Devin glared at Lily as she passed.

She opened the door to find Leo holding a transparent bag in front of his face with two tomatoes covering his eyes.

"Hello? Hello? Is anybody there? I can't see you," he said with feigned worry.

"You keep playin' and you *will* have two swollen eyes," Lily responded.

Leo lowered the tomatoes and flashed a giant grin.

"Fresh vegetables, right out my garden."

"Really? Your garden uses Jackson Market bags too?"

"Wha—I am insulted. But you know I'd grow them if I could, right?"

Lily snatched the bag from Leo's hand and turned toward the kitchen.

"Thank you," she announced in a sing-song cadence while waving her finger in the air.

Leo closed the apartment door and held up his utility bag.

"Brought my tools—rescue team on the premises," he said.

Leo leaned against Devin's door frame.

"Hey big man, how's my favorite nephew?"

Devin didn't look up from his desk. Wispy white smoke rose from his fingers and passed over his hair as he melted solder to a circuit board of electronic components.

"Look at you! Little Thomas Edison, inventing all this—"

"Tesla," Devin interrupted.

Leo paused, "Say what? Tesla?"

"Edison was a fool," Devin said, never breaking his concentration.

"All right. Just playin'. We can go with Tesla."

Leo left Devin's doorway and approached Lily in the kitchen.

"Little man is something else," he said to Lily.

"Mmm-hmm," Lily smirked.

"Which one's the problem child here?" Leo said, motioning at the cabinets.

"Down here. Just pops open."

Leo squatted and opened the door.

"Me and Gracie can take care of this."

"Gracie?"

Leo held up a short carpenter's level.

"Yep, Gracie ... don't worry, she's on the level."

Lily groaned and nudged Leo with her foot, pushing him off balance into a sitting position.

"Hey, hey! Expensive equipment here. And my tools are too."

Leo checked the doors and cabinet frame for level. He ran his hand along the inside of the cabinet. He swung the door in small arcs and listened for creaking. He closed the door, then tugged it open.

"Huh," he said, "everything seems normal. Is there a service elevator or anything on this side of the building?"

"Nope, everything is on the other side. This is the dead end of the building."

"So weird, it's almost like air pressure, or maybe a vibration is opening it. I'd guess an elevator or something. There is that train outside, but it's a block away. Hmmm."

"Yeah, I don't know. But one thing I do know is it's creeping me out."

Leo stood and leaned toward Lily to whisper, "How's he doing in school, getting along all right?"

"You know," she responded with a shrug.

"Roger been sending payments after the lawyer thing?"

"He did, for a little while. I don't expect much—never the best role model."

"I'm sorry, I hate to see this. Dad would have never treated Mom like this. There's something about setting a good male example, even if you are basically a jerk."

"At least Devin isn't getting that negative influence."

• • •

LILY REACHED OVER DEVIN'S SHOULDER to serve him a paper plate holding two plain hot dogs and potato chips. Devin immediately began to eat.

Lily served Leo the same and pointed at a bowl of tomato slices.

"Help yourself to some home-grown tomatoes," she said.

"Awww, yeah! Better than Christmas dinner at the Walnut Room!" he said while nestling tomato slices into his hot dogs.

"Ha," Lily said as she sat.

"Hey, little man," Leo said, "you gettin' on with anybody at school? Got any new friends, maybe a girl who likes you?"

"Leo, please," Lily interjected.

"What? Just chattin'. He's getting to be that age, you know, and he's not exactly an ugly duckling."

"Certainly true, takes after me," she said, stroking her hair.

Leo laughed.

"I made a friend," Devin said.

Lily and Leo stopped laughing and turned toward Devin, sharing a moment of silence.

Leo slowly spread a wide grin and motioned toward Devin, "See? He's making progress. Good for you, little man."

Devin noticed that Leo's smile was the same as his mother's, although she didn't show it much.

"Devin, I didn't know you made a friend," Lily said.

Devin looked into the kitchen and nodded.

"Baby, tell me. In one of your classes?"

"In the building."

"In the building?" Lily said surprised, "In our apartment building? Who did you meet in the building?"

"That's cool," Leo said with a raised thumb, "somebody in the building is cool."

"Devin, who did you meet?" Lily asked again.

"I don't know his name," Devin said with a shoulder shrug. He'd never thought to ask.

"You don't know his name? Well, where does he live?"

Devin remained silent.

"Baby, where does he live?" she said more firmly.

"Three twelve."

"Well, that's cool," Leo interjected, "right on this floor."

"Why didn't you tell me? I need to know these things," Lily scolded.

Devin shrugged.

Lily glared at Devin in disbelief, but he had resumed eating his hot dog.

"This is awesome, making good progress, y'all," Leo said.

In the kitchen, the lower cabinet door popped open, swinging with a slow creak.

Lily twisted in her seat at the sound.

Leo approached the cabinet and dropped to his knees to look inside. He tipped his head sideways, then nearly inverted. Devin found Leo's twisted position amusing.

"Man, I don't see nothing."

Leaning in further, he grabbed the countertop for stability

only to receive a freezing jolt through his hand.

"Ah!" he exclaimed as he jumped, "What is *that*?"

Lily hurried over and placed her palm on the countertop, but the cold was gone.

"And it does that, too," she said, sliding her palm around the surface.

"How'd it get cold like that?"

"I have no idea."

Devin averted his eyes from the kitchen and back to his plate.

• • •

LILY STEPPED OUT OF THE BATHROOM with wet hair from the shower. The long wedge of light stretching across the hallway from Devin's desk lamp went dark.

"You wrapping it up for the night?" she called out.

Lily folded a throw blanket and laid it on the arm of the couch. She turned to find Devin standing motionless behind her.

"Oh!" she screamed out. "Don't do that, baby! What are you doing?"

"It was me," Devin said.

"I know, you scared me to death. Lord."

"The kitchen cabinet. It was me."

"What do you mean, baby?"

Devin held up the small circuit board he had been assembling and pressed a red button. The cabinet door in the kitchen swung open.

"How'd you do that? It was you the whole time?" she asked as she approached the kitchen.

Lily knelt in front of the open cabinet. A partially obscured tiny metal box was mounted inside. A spool of copper wire encased a protruding cylinder. A flat cable connected to a second mounted circuit board.

"What is this thing?"

Devin closed the door. He pressed the button and the door swung open again.

"It's a solenoid. Like a doorbell," he said.

Lily closed the cabinet door.

"Oh, God, I can't believe you invented a ghost like that. Didn't know your little Einstein brain had such a sense of humor." She smiled and squeezed Devin's shoulder.

Devin turned away but stopped after three steps. There was one more detail he needed to make clear.

"Just a prank. Leo doesn't need to come by anymore," he said.

Devin lifted the circuit board above his head and pressed the button again. The door popped open as he scurried back to his bedroom.

"Unreal," Lily said as she closed the cabinet door.

• • •

LEO PACED AROUND HIS APARTMENT with the phone pressed against his ear.

"Hey, hey! It's me. Something's been bothering me since I left.

"No way," Leo said, "There was no circuit board mounted in there, nowhere, there was nothing. He must have put it there after I left.

"I don't know. But check this out, when I was leaving today, some guy in the lobby saw my tool bag and asked if they were still fixing up the unit where that kid died.

"Yep, he said a kid died in apartment three-twelve, told me the kid's mom smashed his head on the countertop and shoved him into the bottom cabinet where he died. I remember hearing about it on the news, had no idea where it was.

"I know it's horrible, but I need you to do something. Listen to me. Open up your front door.

"I'm serious, Lily, do it now.

"Okay, what number is on your door?

"Right, three-thirteen. And the unit across the hall?

"Yep, three-eleven. And the units next to you?

"Exactly. There is no three-twelve because that was *your* apartment before they changed the number.

"That's right, that kid died in three-twelve, in *your* apartment, in your cabinet.

"I know, but hold on, here's the part I really don't like—

"He's what? Why does he have my hammer? Just tell him to wait, tell him you need a minute. I think the kid that died in your apartment … is Devin's new friend. I think he's—

"Lily, what was that?

"Hello?

"Lily?"

PHOTOGRAPH FROM THE FUTURE

L AST WEEKEND WHILE CLEANING out an old, forgotten trunk, I found an envelope that I had misplaced for some time. It had my father's handwriting in blue ink:

Visit me in the future, let's open this together. Love, Dad.

I remember when he gave me that envelope, it was my sixteenth birthday—and it wasn't entirely out of character for him. I asked him what was inside and he beamed, "It's a photograph from the future!"

"When, exactly, in the future should we open this?"

He assured me I would know when the time was right.

"Why can't I just open it in five minutes, which would technically be in the future?"

He said I could open it now if I wished, but the magic of the photo would be meaningless. I trusted in him, so I waited.

MY FATHER LOVED TO DISPENSE his magic. It wasn't card tricks or silver rings or rabbits in hats; he knew things about the future, things he shouldn't really know. He knew the name of the girl I would marry, ten years before I met her. He knew the exact date my daughter would be born, a year before we even knew we were expecting. He knew dementia would ravage my mother. He knew what her last words would be.

He just knew things.

OCCASIONALLY, HE CLAIMED TO HAVE actual items from the future, like the photograph.

I remember one summer day he said to me, just a little kid, "I have a coin from the future, do you want to see it?"

Of course I wanted to see it, it was from the future.

He pulled a shiny coin from his pocket and placed it in my palm. He raised his eyebrows and widened his grin, "What do you think?"

I leaned in for closer inspection, but wasn't convinced, "This looks like a normal coin."

His smile faded, "Oh my, it sure does."

He paused, then asked, "What year is it, right now?"

I told him and he nodded in agreement, "Yes it is."

He paused again, then asked, "What year is this coin?"

I inspected the coin but didn't see a date, so I turned it over and saw that the date was for the upcoming year.

Amazed, I exclaimed, "Whoa, it is from the future!"

I ALWAYS WANTED TO BE LIKE my father. He was buoyant and youthful, clever and patient. He always brought people joy. *Always*.

But I never understood the source of his magic.

In my early teens, I had the chore of mowing our yard. Our neighbor was an old, widowed man who was friendly with my father. One day I wanted to try and mimic my father's magic, so when I finished our yard, I continued on and mowed our neighbor's yard too.

When I was done I went up to his porch and knocked on his door. When he finally answered, I greeted him with respect and asked if I could mow his yard on this hot, uncomfortable day. He agreed with subdued delight. I told him that I would also be using magic to get it done faster than humanly possible.

He said, "Well ... magic is fine, but don't hurt my flowers," and closed the door.

I waited a few seconds and knocked again. He soon opened the door.

"Did you need something else?"

I told him that I had finished with my magic mowing and that his yard was done.

He stepped out on the porch and looked around in amazement, "That's not humanly possible!"

I beamed a giant smile and announced, "Yes sir, It's magic!" and skipped back to my house. I'm pretty sure he gave my father a wink, who'd been watching the whole time.

MANY YEARS LATER, MY YOUNG daughter and I were driving through town and I asked her, "Do you want to see a car from the future?"

Of course she did, it was from the future.

I turned into a car dealership and parked. We walked across the lot of cars, up to a shiny new one. I held out my hands and said, "Presenting ... a car from the future!"

She said, "Dad, this looks like a normal car."

I knelt down and cupped her shoulder, "What year is it, right now?"

She told me and I nodded in agreement, "Yes it is."

I stood back up and tapped on the window sticker showing this to be a model from next year, "What does this say, right there?"

Her jaw dropped, "Wow, it is from the future!"

I was proud to be following in the footsteps of my magic father, being clever and youthful, and bringing joy to others.

But something always nagged at me, there was something

about his magic that seemed different from my lackluster imitations, something just out of reach; like he was actually magical.

· · ·

WHEN I FOUND THAT OLD ENVELOPE, I was stunned to be holding it again. Tracing my father's handwriting with my finger, I became a bit saddened and embarrassed that I had misplaced it for so long.

Visit me in the future, let's open this together, it said, so I decided it was time to visit him and we could finally open it together.

I called my daughter to ask if she could help. I've been having some trouble with my vision and she, again, agreed to drive me there. When we arrived, she told me to go on ahead, she had to make a quick phone call and would be along soon.

I've never been a person who converses out loud at the cemetery, but this day was different, this day I had things to say. I felt the need to explain what happened with the envelope, how I had misplaced it for so long, and how I felt sick to my stomach that we didn't get to open it together. I told him that for a long time I tried with great desperation to guess what was in the photograph from the future, but refused to open it without him.

Once, I predicted that he would probably replace the envelope with a newer one, so that the photo showed something in the future, relative to when he gave it to me. Clever me made a slight opening in the envelope and slid the coin from the future into it, then sealed it with tape. Later, when the envelope and tape never changed and I could still feel the coin inside, I changed my mind. I was certain that he had probably taken a photo of a fake newspaper with some crazy date hundreds of years in the future.

Regardless, the envelope had remained sealed all these years, the photo unseen.

I slid my finger under the flap and broke the seal. I paused.

What if I was supposed to open it right away, that day on my birthday, and whatever big surprise he had planned was ruined? I felt awful.

I reached in and pulled out the photo, but didn't recognize the image. It showed an old man standing near flowers, I couldn't imagine who it could have been. Maybe just some crooked old man he knew from long ago.

Then I removed the coin from the envelope. It was still shiny. But I couldn't make out the small writing.

My daughter approached, asking, "What's that?"

I handed her the coin and the photo. I explained what they were, the photograph from the future and the coin from the future. I described how I came to possess them both. I told her how the envelope had been misplaced and why we were here today.

She looked closely at the coin.

"This coin was sealed in *that* envelope?"

"Yes," I said, "I just opened it."

She turned it over in her hand to look at the back, then read the date on the front again.

"Dad, this coin is dated from *next year*. How did …"

She studied the photo of the old man standing near flowers holding an envelope. Her eyes moved on to me, inspecting my clothes, shoes, and hat.

"Dad …" she began

With hesitation, she continued, "This photo is of you. From today. This is you, standing right here, right now."

She flipped the photo over to discover writing. She handed it to me and I immediately recognized my father's distinctive handwriting:

> *To my son, the true source of my magic.*
> *Thank you for opening the envelope with me today, together.*
> *And thank you for visiting me so many times in this future*
> *of yours.*

I became overwhelmed with emotion—sadness, happiness, relief; all mixing into a melancholy calm.

I missed my father immensely. I missed his buoyancy and cleverness. I missed his great smile.

But even after all this time apart, he was still bringing me joy. Still bringing joy like he always had. *Always*.

DRAGONS

DRAGONS, THERE ARE dragons, you say.
Lurking and plotting wrath and revenge.
Writhing behind castles,
seething at our presence.

Butterflies, these are butterflies, I say.
Flittering and seeking clover and sage.
Resting upon sunflowers,
ignoring our presence.

Condemn, be distressed, you say.
For they have fire and hateful notions.
Soaring terror of the air,
despised by men of arrogance.

Rejoice, be jubilant, I say.
For these have colors and graceful arcs.
Transient flower gardens of the air,
loved by men of humility.

Afford them steel, you say.
Afford them arrows.
Sharpen all blades
to end their lives.

Afford them love, I say.
Afford them concord.
Soften your heart
to end your malice.

If your dragons come, I will not see them.
I will be entranced by the colors and grace of flittering joy.
Lest spoiling what livens me with what burdens you,
I will not look.

Dragons may burn and cease me, but I will not watch.
I will be content, having obtained what I've sought.
You may burn and cease as well, but you will certainly watch.
You will be content that you, too, obtained what you sought.

APRIL

THE TOPS OF THE WEEDS tickled the spread-out arms of the kids. With each step through the long grass, insects fluttered into the warm mid-afternoon air. Jackie hummed as he picked up a fist-sized rock and struck the steel support cable of the looming radio tower. A metallic clang raced up to the flashing red light and back down again. Its whipping song continued to pulse several more times, fading with each oscillation.

April followed closely as Jackie forged a path through the expansive field. On some days after school, the two would meet in April's back yard at the edge of the radio tower field and create adventures. Bent arms and fingers induced roars from terrifying dinosaurs. A laundry basket became the carriage of a runaway Ferris wheel. The back of April's three-story house became a mountain cliff where ugly giants perched to choose children to eat. Luckily, our brave hero always prevailed and saved the girl on these perilous voyages.

But on this day, Jackie had a different adventure planned.

"I hope Danny isn't in a bad mood," Jackie said as he spun a full circle in the field of weeds. Three steps later he spun again, "I made you a gift—you're gonna like it!"

April smiled and jumped to reach for a passing grasshopper. Jackie continued forward with arms spread, his soaring airplane swerving through stormy clouds.

A NEGLECTED MOBILE HOME came into view. It hid in the shade of a giant tree at the edge of thick woods; vines were overtaking its dirty tan siding. A discarded couch and a three-legged chair lay near a rusty barbecue grill. Two tires were stacked and tall weeds grew through their rimless center. Jackie jumped up to look over a patch of thick bushes.

"My mom isn't home yet, I'll have to be extra nice to Danny," he said.

"Are you sure this is okay? My birthday isn't until tomorrow. Won't it ruin the surprise?"

They slowed their walk as they reached a rusty chain-link fence. Jackie lifted a loose section to let April duck under. Jackie followed and they tiptoed across compacted dirt to hide behind the back of Danny's pickup truck.

Jackie crouched near the tailgate and said, "Danny says we have to go to my grandma's today for the weekend. She's old and cranky and smells like cigarettes. I can't be here for your birthday party. I'm sorry April."

April sat on her heels behind the truck. She held her daisy-patterned dress down over her bent legs and rested her chin on her knees. She picked up a rock and carved a smiley face into the dirt as she said, "That's okay, I know how stinky grandmas are."

Jackie crept upward and peered around the bed of the truck toward the screen door.

"Stay right here while I go ask, I'll be right back."

Jackie opened the screen door at half speed. Tinny applause came from a small TV sitting on a folding chair. A game show host held a microphone up to a bearded contestant and asked where it was he called home.

Danny slept in an outstretched recliner. His wiry thin frame barely filled out his baggy work pants and mechanic shirt. His dirty red Budweiser cap had shifted down his forehead.

Jackie stepped quietly.

Tuscaloosa? Wow! The game show host laughed.

"Excuse me," Jackie said as he tapped Danny's shoulder.

Danny lifted his head with a wobble and turned to look at Jackie through bloodshot eyes.

"Excuse me, Mister Danny, can I go to the woods for a bit?"

Danny turned toward the TV when he heard applause again. He reached up to adjust his cap and looked back at Jackie.

"What for?"

"I forgot something there—last time. I just need to go get it real quick—I'll be right back."

Danny stared through Jackie with glazed eyes.

"You're not hanging out with that rich girl, are you?" he mumbled.

"No, sir."

"Are you packed yet? We're going to grandma's as soon as your mom gets home."

"I know, I'm all ready. I'll come right back."

Danny reacted with a slow blink, then looked down at Jackie's dirty white t-shirt.

"You ain't wearing that dirty thing, change it."

"I will, I promise," Jackie said as he scuttled toward the door.

"Don't make me come get you!" Danny shouted as he crossed his arms and closed his eyes.

The screen door slammed as Jackie jumped off the porch and lifted his bike away from a bent clothesline post. He wheeled the bike around Danny's truck and crouched down next to April.

"We're clear," Jackie said, "You can have the seat."

Jackie straddled the bike near the handlebars and April lifted her foot over the center bar and wiggled herself onto the seat. Jackie carefully turned the bike toward the heavy trees and shuffled his feet on the dirt to pick up speed. Five big steps and he lifted himself to stand on the pedals, squatting up and down on each foot to pick up speed.

The kids had ridden this way before, and April was confident of Jackie's command of his bike. April rested her hands on Jackie's shoulders and imagined she was riding a carousel horse at the county fair. April's smile widened as the wind lifted and tossed her hair.

Jackie considered himself an expert voyager of the woods. He knew which areas of weeds and underbrush had dangerous rocky patches underneath. He knew which ridges to ride as the terrain began its slow fall toward the lake. He knew where the big stalks of weaving poison ivy vines formed giant walls of itchy nightmares.

JACKIE OFTEN PRETENDED HE WAS riding a horse through the trees like the native Indians did when they were the only people on this land. A winding paved road led all the way down to the lake, but Jackie knew the Indians wouldn't have used the road, so he didn't either. There's no adventure in rolling smoothly down the middle of blacktop, and Jackie thrived on adventure.

After navigating through trees and underbrush and poison ivy, the kids slowed as they neared a large boulder in a dense growth of trees. Jackie stopped at the base of the stone and planted his feet to let April step off.

She touched her palm to the stone, finding it to be cool and covered in tiny condensation droplets.

"This is really neat!" April said, "How did it get here?"

"I don't know," Jackie said as he laid down his bike, "but that's not what I wanted to show you. Here, come this way."

Jackie led April past the stone and into a darker area of shade. He jumped over a fallen tree branch and held April's arm for support as her shiny black shoes nearly slipped on the mossy surface. Jackie led April through a dip in the terrain and up to a wall of vines hanging from above.

"These are safe—they're not poison ivy," Jackie said as he grabbed a leaf from the vine and rubbed it between his fingers.

Jackie pulled the vines apart and the two kids stepped through. Just ahead was a small grassy clearing lit up from the sun shining through a break in the tree tops.

"Wow," April said upon seeing the golden soft glow illuminating the emerald grass.

The kids approached and the glow became brighter. Standing in the clearing was an old tree with a distinct right-angle bend three feet off the ground. Three more feet and the tree continued back toward the sky. A long strand of vines had been intentionally wrapped in layers around the tree. Two large leaves and a tuft of weeds were attached just above the second bend. A white ribbon was tied around the skyward section.

"So pretty!" April said, "Did you do this?"

"I decorated it to be a carousel horse for you. I know you love them."

"This is so amazing, Jackie! How did you bend the tree like that?"

"I didn't," Jackie said, "The Indians used to step on trees to mark their paths. This one must have kept growing that way, I guess. It looked like a horse to me and I thought of you."

April sat sidesaddle on the tree and grabbed the white ribbon reigns.

"I love it!" she exclaimed.

April shook the reigns and giggled, "It looks so real. Thank you!"

"I'm glad you like it, I've been—" Jackie began, but paused and turned back in the direction of the giant stone.

"Did you hear that?" he asked as he took two small steps away from April.

"I don't hear anything but pretty birds."

Becoming motionless, Jackie cupped his hands around his ears to magnify the sound. Shortly, he could hear a honking truck horn and his name being yelled.

"Oh no, that's Mister Danny," Jackie said.

He took another step toward the sound, then turned to April with wide eyes.

"Are you sure?" April asked.

Jackie clutched his fists.

"Wait here, I'll go see what he wants. I'll be right back."

Jackie held up his palms to April.

"I'll be back, I'll be *right* back."

Jackie turned toward the sound and ran. *I'll be right back, I'll be right back*, he repeated to himself as he neared the stone. He lifted his bike and rode toward the road. As Jackie reached the blacktop, Danny pulled up with his arm hanging out of the open window.

"Where the hell have you been? Your mom is pissed—I told you not to go anywhere, I told you to stay home!"

"I was just about to come back—I'm done, I'm done."

Danny stepped out of the truck, ripped the bike from Jackie's hands, and flung it into the truck bed.

"Get in!" he shouted.

Jackie stood frozen with his hands pointing back toward where April sat waiting.

"I just need a second to—"

"Get in the *damn* truck, Jackie! I'm sick of your bullshit," Danny yelled as he raised his open palm above his shoulder.

Jackie ducked to avoid getting slapped. He ran around the truck and fumbled with the handle to get inside. He pulled the door shut and pinned himself near the window crank, just out of Danny's reach. Fear and tears formed in his eyes at the thought of leaving April alone in the woods.

Danny turned the truck around and with a monstrous engine growl, peeled out on the roadside spewing dirt and leaves and squealing a tire as it hit the blacktop.

• • •

"AREN'T YOU DONE yet?" Mrs. Abbott called to her husband from inside the garage.

He stood next to the car, tightening the brackets on a rooftop carrier.

"Almost," he said, "I just need to—"

"Hurry up," she interrupted, "clouds are coming in. We need to get there while it's still sunny."

He sighed as he lifted the first of two kayaks to the top of the car.

"I'm working on it," he mumbled.

As he tightened the straps around the kayak, he glanced toward the end of his street. The blinking light on the radio tower caught his attention. His eyes drifted downward, noticing the three-story house whose yard backed up against the large grassy field. A silver Mercedes sedan pulled into the driveway. He stopped to watch as a young woman in a tight black skirt stepped out of the car and opened the trunk. His eyes were fixed as she bent forward to remove two department store shopping bags.

"What are you looking at, Jonathan?" his wife asked in a contemptuous tone, having suddenly appeared next to him.

"Nothing."

"I suppose you're merely admiring the house, hmmm? Such an *interesting* tower—she's married with a kid, you know."

"No, I don't know anything about that family."

"Could you just finish so we can get going? Your own daughter is waiting."

AS THE LAST STRAP OF THE SECOND kayak was tightened, Mrs. Abbott clicked the seatbelt of her daughter's toddler seat.

"I packed some sandwiches for later," she said to her husband, "I didn't know what you wanted so just I made peanut butter."

"You know I hate peanut butter. And why do we need sandwiches—how long do you think we're going to be on mosquito lake?"

"We'll be there as long as we want to be there," she scolded.

"But *she* doesn't care about kayaking, and I absolutely *hate* going into woods."

"Some child psychologist you are. For all the money you make, you have exactly zero empathy for how to make someone feel happy. Can we go now?"

AS JONATHAN BACKED OUT of his driveway and slowed the car, the tower light flashed in his rearview mirror. He straightened his arching back until the three-story house and Mercedes came into view. He held his eyes on the car's reflection as he drove away.

They passed expensive SUVs and sports cars, custom landscaping with fountains and waterfalls. They followed the road around the private golf course until the radio tower came into view again.

"Do you know where the entrance is?" Jonathan asked.

"Unreal. You don't even know where we're going?" her words dripped with contempt.

"I told you, I have no desire whatsoever to go. I hate the woods, I hate the lake, I hate living here."

"Oh, again with the '*I hate it here*'. This is the best neighborhood in town. What, do you want to live in one of those poor-people mobile homes?"

Jonathan clenched his jaw and slowly shook his head, "I think I can figure it out."

AS THE FAMILY DROVE INTO the forest preserve entrance, Jonathan squinted and said, "Welcome to murder forest, next stop … mosquito lake."

His wife quipped back, "I brought bug spray, mister Happy Joy."

The road narrowed and wound through the shade of tall trees. Jonathan leaned and looked upward, shaking his head in displeasure. As they slowed for a sharp turn, he noticed the huge boulder amongst the thick trees. He did a double-take, then looked again in the rearview mirror.

"That's strange."

"What?" his wife asked.

"Nothing … I thought I saw something back there past that big rock."

"I didn't see any big rock. What are you talking about?"

Jonathan didn't respond but twisted his neck to try and catch another glimpse.

"Keep your eyes on the road!" she said, "We don't need to get into a traumatic—"

She stopped mid-sentence and pointed to the back seat with her thumb, hiding it from their daughter.

Jonathan slowed the car as they entered a series of three sharp bends in the road, his face tight with disdain.

GRAVEL CRUNCHED UNDER TIRES as Jonathan backed into an open spot. As he unstrapped the first kayak from the top of the car, his wife secured a life preserver on their daughter. He took the kayak to the dock and placed it on the launch rollers. After his wife was seated, he lifted his daughter and set her in the kayak and tussled her hair. He placed the paddle into his wife's hands and helped her push off the dock.

"Go on ahead, I'll catch up," he said.

"Hurry up. You'd better not let me tip over."

"Relax, the water's calm, you'll be fine. I'll be out in a few minutes."

Jonathan stood with his hands on his hips as watched the kayak drift away. He heard his wife baby-talking their daughter, telling her about all the colorful fish they were going to see on their big adventure.

Colorful fish? he thought, *This ain't the tropics, lady.*

He headed back to the car, but instead of removing the second kayak, he sat and drove away. He navigated through the three sharp bends and stopped at the curve where he had seen the giant boulder.

He parked off the road and stepped out. The shade was thick with humidity and loud insects fluttered and taunted him from every direction. He approached the boulder and touched his fingertips to the condensation and cool surface. A nervous jolt shot up his arm and he jerked his hand away. He brought his fingers to his chest to wipe the moisture from his fingers.

The echoing sound of a young girl's giggle filled the air, swirling around Jonathan's ears. He crept around the stone and heard the laughter originating from the darker area of the woods. He swallowed hard.

I hate this, I hate this.

As if they developed courage of their own, his feet carried him into the heavier shade. He stepped over the branch of a fallen tree with a large stride. When his foot touched the ground he nearly lost his balance from the slippery moss.

Jonathan's feet carried him across a dip in the terrain and up to a wide wall of vines. Echoing laughter seeped from beyond the vines. He picked up a long stick and pulled the vines aside to step through.

Fifty feet ahead the sun broke through with a soft golden glow onto a grassy clearing. There was movement, something was illuminated.

As he continued toward the clearing he noticed a young girl in a flowered summer dress sitting on the bent tree. Facing away from Jonathan, she rocked back and forth and hummed a happy melody. He stopped, his nervous eyes scanning the woods. She seemed to be alone.

Upon entering the clearing, he stepped on a brittle branch and it snapped. Jonathan froze. The girl tilted her head.

"I'm so glad you're back, Jackie," she said with innocent relief, "I've been waiting."

"Hello?" Jonathan called out, "I'm sorry, are you lost?"

"No, silly," she replied with a giggle that echoed around his head.

"Are you okay?"

"I've been waiting for you," she said.

"You're waiting—is someone coming?" Jonathan asked.

"Of course, Jackie, I'm waiting for *you*."

A chill crept across his neck, goosebumps rose on his arms.

"My name's ... Jonathan," he said.

"Jonathan?"

"Yes."

She giggled.

"Jonathan? I thought only your stinky grandma called you that. Why don't you want to be called Jackie anymore?" she said in a deepening voice.

She stood from the tree and lowered her head, her hair falling across her face.

"Are you still telling lies, Jackie?" she taunted, "Do you lie about things from your past?"

Jonathan stood frozen, unable to blink.

The girl turned her head to face Jonathan. Her skin was pale and purple—her eyes colorless. Her neck was slit open and the front of her dress was covered in dark, sticky, coagulated blood.

She began an awkward and slow walk toward Jonathan.

"Jackie, you never came back," her voice became deeper.

"No, no—I ..."

Her pace was slow and she growled louder.

"You never came back."

"No. April, I tried. April ... I, I—" Jonathan stammered.

She sprinted at incredible speed with her hands outstretched, immediately reaching Jonathan. Her hands formed a strangling grip around his throat, knocking him down. She kneeled on his chest and sneered with black, rotten teeth. She pressed her face up to his as black slime oozed from her lips and landed in his mouth.

"Jackie!" she bellowed in a deep beastly growl, "You never came back!"

SPIDER POINTE

A VERY LONG TIME AGO, during an era of hope, a determined wagon train of westward-bound pioneers crossed prairie grass plains and traversed muddy rivers. They fought snowstorms and endured insect swarms. Each step forward was driven by the desire to start anew and was supported by the grit to withstand Mother Nature's most daunting resistance.

One warm spring day, the wagons of tired travelers entered a clear, flat valley between steep foothills covered in thick woods. A harsh winter had drained spirits and left many of the families despondent over the loss of friends and loved ones. Regret about persisting had been seeping into weary hearts, but this newfound beautiful land restored their waning hope. A lush blanket of green fields spread wide across the valley floor and touched the hills of woodland. Wildflowers dotted the landscape and their sweet fragrances danced in the warm air. A sturdy river traversing through the valley was so clear, a man could count the scales on the schools of fish. The steep hills stood strong and wrapped around the valley like a protective mother's hug. This is where they settled.

High in the hills on a treeless bluff, an unusual protrusion of rocks thrust outward and upward in the majestic shape of a crown. It didn't fit the geological features of the hills and bearing such a unique look only contributed to the magnificence of the valley. The town elders found inspiration from the shape and stature of the bluff and dubbed it King's Pointe.

THE FOLLOWING YEAR ON A CLEAR summer day, a young boy playing with a rolling hoop near the woods saw movement on the ledge protruding from the rocks of King's Pointe. He later claimed he saw a spider that stared back at him with menacing beady eyes, plotting as a hunter would. He was never the same again; his nights were restless and he rarely ventured out of his home to play.

He was ridiculed by the elders and other families, claiming the boy must have the eyes of a hawk to see a spider at such a distance to King's Pointe from the valley floor. Henceforth, he was referred to as Hawkeye, a mocking nickname from the townspeople that he loathed for life.

Hawkeye stood firm to the truth of his story, knowing deep in his heart what he had seen. One day, as a maturing man and the newly elected mayor, he officially changed the name of that rock formation to Spider Pointe; a satisfying vengeance for a life of hurtful taunting. To the townspeople of this new generation, Spider Pointe seemed like a reasonable, fresh name, and an issue unworthy of bringing to argument.

• • •

NONE OF THE TOWNSPEOPLE HAD ever actually seen the top of Spider Pointe. The steepness of the rocky facade, their lack of climbing skill, and the quality of their modest footwear made the climb an impossible feat.

Over time, boys became men, and masculinity has a way of provoking a man to prove his physical prowess. A challenge arose amongst these cocksure men about who could be the first to conquer Spider Pointe. A strong blacksmith declared he could easily win and forged a pair of custom spikes which he secured around his boots. Intimidated by these amazing climbing spikes, the others allowed the blacksmith first attempt.

He fared well with his natural strength and supplemental footwear, but tragedy followed on that day. The blacksmith climbed far enough to reach the stone shelf and outstretched his arms to support himself as his feet searched for stability. The effort of the climb was exhausting and he paused to collect his breath. Stories say that he screamed as he fell to his death, but descendants of the men who were there that day, watching from below, swear that the blacksmith started screaming many seconds before he actually fell.

Attempts at reaching Spider Pointe became illegal soon afterward and the town erected a marker where the blacksmith fell and gave it the foreboding name of Red Rocks. After becoming damaged one year, the sign was never replaced. But the story of the blacksmith and Red Rocks lived on in gruesome lore.

• • •

OVER THE NEXT ONE HUNDRED AND FIFTY years, the town would continue to grow as a hub of vigor and optimism. The incursion of railroad enabled profitable trade, an upstream dam brought hydroelectric power, and the founding of a university brought commerce. The school was founded by naturalists who believed in educating people about the goodness of nature and how nature adapts and survives.

THE LATTER PART OF the twentieth century brought an increased interest in fitness and exercise. Many university students took to the hills for recreational hiking and camping, which in turn attracted more students to the school. A formal designation of named trails was established and the woods became more friendly for inexperienced nature lovers.

Increased exploration of the terrain revealed these hills contained a large number of hidden cave openings, believed to lead to an interconnected cave system. Formed into the limestone from glacier activity over millions of years, the openings had been well-hidden beneath thick underbrush, covered by a literal blanket of earth-tone camouflage.

An unfortunate side effect of the increased traffic into the woods was an increased number of missing hikers. The openings to the caves were known to be irregular and inherently dangerous, but for the adventurous, these caves brought the potential for enormous braggadocio. It became common reasoning that the missing hikers had likely perished after pushing too far into the formidable cave structures.

. . .

THE BEGINNING OF THE TWENTY-FIRST century brought new technology that was adapted for hikers: persistent signal transmitters to serve as location beacons. The school strongly encouraged everyone heading into the hills to have a tracking device in their gear at all times.

Locating missing hikers was a reactionary and slow process initiated only when someone had been reported missing for several days. A search team would be dispatched into the hills and slow combing of thick growth and underbrush could take weeks.

Usually, the hikers were never found, as forward progress into the caves was nearly impossible. Regardless, there were never beacon signals emanating from within to warrant the risk. The devices were created to be mostly indestructible and contained batteries lasting many years, but the signal detectors were limited and no match for the complex cave structures.

A DECADE OR SO LATER, A GROUP of engineering students at the university developed a beacon-detecting system that could possibly surmount the problem of the caves. Combining radio receivers, infrared cameras, and sonar technology mounted to drones, detection and visibility into the stone would be greatly increased. When used in conjunction with multiple drones flying simultaneously, triangulation in three-dimensional real-time was a reality.

Preliminary testing around the campus showed great promise, and the team was ready to take their work to the hills. Spacing the drones at lateral intervals and at varying altitudes, the imaging team made adjustments from their control truck until their sensors lit up with several existing beacons. Their existing three-dimensional model of the surface infused with the beacon signal mappings confirmed what they had always suspected, the cave system was huge and a few beacons were transmitting from deep within.

But as the pilots moved the matrix of drones further toward Spider Pointe, the number of beacon signals increased significantly. A drone equipped for video revealed the long flat ledge actually jutted out from another cave entrance. The beacon drones had indicated a large number of signals coming from this exact spot, so the camera was flown inside to provide visibility.

A short distance into the cave, where the ledge met the back wall, a meter-high mound of moist and messy brown ooze spread about. The monitoring team identified it as a gigantic mass of spider excrement. As they hypothesized how it got there, the drone was knocked out of the air and all signals were lost.

The team increased sonar and infrared on three nearby drones and jaws dropped when they imaged a large source of movement inside the cave. Increasing resolution revealed the source to be shaped like a gigantic spider, much larger than an automobile. And dozens of beacons were transmitting from within the pile of excrement.

Sensitivity was increased on all detectors and the full army of drones dispersed out above the hills. To their horror, the team detected many more of the creatures spread throughout the hills, hiding in the treetops and blending into underbrush. Watching and waiting, these were patient hunters.

Panic set in at the university as they were suddenly faced with a dilemma—reveal the truth about the grim danger awaiting in the woods, or provide a false narrative to protect the survival of the very natural habitat they were founded to preserve. The official statements from the university claimed that the cave system had begun collapsing and the trails had become increasingly unstable. But a truth of this magnitude could not be kept silent for long.

THE CITY EXISTS BECAUSE OF the natural beauty of the woods and the valley, and the majestic crown of King's Pointe. The ancestors could not have settled a more pleasing landscape. But one small boy, many years ago, warned the people of danger, and his caution was ridiculed. Now the woods have been permanently closed to the public and the overwhelming fear of this once enticing nature cripples an overgrown city.

But, luckily, one of the beneficial traits of evolution and nature is adaptation and survival; if prey stops coming to the predator, the predator will seek the prey.

And the prey ultimately, and always, ends up here, with us, at Spider Pointe.

PINE

Pine: An American Narrative
by Ellen Blakeley
Headington, Oxfordshire, England
Penned 1910

EVERY GAZE UPON HER sleeping baby filled Mrs. Mitchell with the tranquility of a sipped glass of Vin Mariani. Each careful stroke of her littlest finger across the baby's hair—as fine and soft to make the down of a new gosling jealous—brought her a smile, a satisfaction held for hours on end.

The war had brought difficult stresses on the younger wives throughout the county. Some with no labour skills were suddenly thrust into banal duties of milking, chopping, and harvesting as their farms required. Their husbands had been away long enough to allow darkness to seep into their hearts, that which follows when hope wanes. But Mrs. Mitchell held no compassion for those who had become farmers without negroes to labour and toil. Her only concession was to care for her baby.

• • •

TEN YEARS PRIOR, MRS. MITCHELL was but a blossoming child in Savannah, full of wonder and jaunty disposition. Her father was claimed as one of the many successful exporters of cotton flowing from the southern states to New England and Europe. It was here that she would be courted among the tall pines by her future husband, a specimen of hearty stature, the son of a highly respected military man.

The newlyweds settled into a less populous county where Mister Mitchell's competency in financial affairs was highly recruited by the sawmill. Missing the bustle of the big city, Mrs. Mitchell encouraged her husband to let a residence above the chemist's shop overlooking the town square. Her view from the window allowed stealthful observations—the colourful stumblings from pubs with heads held high in song, as well as those who entered the courthouse with heads held in sullen shame.

Shortly after their baby was born, Mister Mitchell answered his call to uphold the values of the newly-formed Confederacy. Mrs. Mitchell made her husband promise that he would help the war to end swiftly with victory and he shall be along home in what will surely seem but a fortnight. Mrs. Mitchell had no labourious concerns, and walking with the baby and the optimism of her husband's return filled her days with buoyancy.

· · ·

MONTHS AND THE UNION prevailed and Mrs. Mitchell no longer held hope so forward in her disposition. The young mother less often left her home and had become a sight of diminished constitution within a begrimed overcoat and hair disheveled without apparent desire for combs. Patrons ambling on the square below often observed the melancholy Mrs. Mitchell rocking her baby in the window above the chemist.

On a midday Tuesday, shortly after dinner break, and shortly after the courthouse doors were reopened to a few men shifting on their nervous feet, a rap came to Mrs. Mitchell's door. She lay the baby into the lacework-trimmed cradle and rushed with utmost haste and hush to intercept her visitor from striking the door again.

Mrs. Mitchell opened the door to find her rotund landlord, Mister Krantz, humbly bowed with his hands before him, nervously turning the brim of his felt hat.

"Mister Krantz, how untimely of you to raise such commotion upon my door, as the baby has just been laid to rest after a most difficult morning," Mrs. Mitchell scolded in hushed tones.

"My sincerest apologies, Mrs. Mitchell. I did not know your circumstances, but should have interpreted the quietness of your home as an indicator of your baby's condition."

"I would most candidly agree, sir."

"Again, please accept my apologies for the intrusion," Mister Krantz surrendered.

"Well! What is the emergency you bring to my door at this inconvenient time? Is the chemist's shop below consumed in fire and smoke?"

"No ma'am, all is well within the building. There is no pending emergency requiring evacuation. I've come to you, in as humble a manner as I can wear, to request payment of the rent past due. I have not received the agreed-upon amount for months now, and in order to meet my own financials, I must approach you today with this appeal."

"Rubbish ..." Mrs. Mitchell began before raising a finger to Mister Krantz and bending an ear toward the interior of her home.

"Surely you have forgotten," she continued with lesser volume, "my husband arranged for all rent and other transactions to occur in his absence. It is not proper to burden a woman with such things. Please check your ledger for I am certain you are confounded in this matter."

"I do not wish to bring about undue arraignment, but I have doubly checked my accounting and must adhere to my conclusions of dereliction."

"Mister Krantz, I again assure you of my husband's provisioning. In fact, a post I received from him just three days ago confirms the claims I put forth to you."

"Mrs. Mitchell, if it would not be of severe inconvenience, would you mind if I were to read his words for myself, with my only intention of clarification?"

"How dare you, Mister Krantz! Letters between my husband and I hold discussions personal between us, and most certainly reveal claims of affection that are not to be shared with parties uninvolved!" she scolded.

Mister Krantz gripped his hat with firm embarrassment.

"Of course, Mrs. Mitchell, of course. I will retreat to my ledger and work to find the errors in my accounting. Please accept my sincerest apologies, and I hope my visit has not disturbed your baby's peaceful slumber."

"Good day, Mister Krantz," Mrs. Mitchell spoke as she closed her door unto the hallway.

Mrs. Mitchell resumed to her chair by the window, pushing a loose blanket into a tighter tuck around the baby.

"Preposterous," she whispered to herself.

• • •

THE NEXT MORNING, SHOPKEEPERS swept away yellow pollen from the walkways and freshly cut planks of pine were unloaded from a wagon. Mrs. Mitchell paced about her residence holding the baby wrapped in a secure soft blanket.

"Shhhhhh," she whispered in soothing repetition.

In a much more respectful manner than the day before, a small tapping came on Mrs. Mitchell's door, which she opened with the utmost care to find the landlord's wife smiling with quiet grace.

"Mrs. Krantz," Mrs. Mitchell began in a whisper, "I wasn't expecting you."

"I am aware of my unexpected inconvenience, but you must take my visit, I plead of you."

Mrs. Mitchell, being more fond of Mrs. Krantz than her husband, caressed the blanket around the baby and said, "Very well."

Mrs. Krantz entered and stood near the small secretary desk to rest her hand on the hutch.

"Give me a moment to settle the baby into the cradle," Mrs. Mitchell whispered, "I hope not to erase my gains in sleep after a very difficult time overnight. Please excuse me."

"No, please, stay here with me, I will not be of nuisance to the baby's sleep. You will both be undisturbed in my presence."

Mrs. Mitchell caressed the blanket again, and said, "Very well."

"I must offer apologies for the scruples of my husband yesterday, his manners are most unrefined and his delivery most uncouth."

"It is easy to fault a countryman who has not the manners of a refined city woman such as myself, and of which I am sure you are as well."

"Your heedfulness is strong, Mrs. Mitchell."

The women shared a pretentious smile as would an empress being handed the list of cheap wines within the local pub.

Mrs. Mitchell turned toward the kitchen and said, "Please, stay for cider, give me company while the baby sleeps."

"Of course, Mrs. Mitchell, you are most kind."

Mrs. Krantz gave pause at the desk and browsed over the home of Mrs. Mitchell. Considering the lack of her husband and the constraints of a small child, things were reasonably coherent and undisturbed. Mrs. Krantz noticed three post envelopes stacked on the desk and her own acquaintance with military transmit allowed her to conclude them to be from her husband away at war.

But the topmost letter, with a different presentation, had not been returned to its more formal envelope. Although bearing a fold and partially concealed, the letter closing was conspicuous to Mrs. Krantz and evidenced itself from the Confederate Army themselves. She found this queer and although having strong desires to open the letter further, she made her way to meet Mrs. Mitchell.

Upon entering the kitchen, Mrs. Krantz found Mrs. Mitchell cradling the covered baby, swaying slowly at the hips, humming a soft lullaby into the blanket. She had yet to set out any cups of cider for herself or her guest.

"Is everything well?" Mrs. Krantz asked.

Mrs. Mitchell spun her head and said, "The baby has been fussing exceedingly, it is taking a while to bring settle. My apologies if I allowed you to hear my efforts and frustration."

"I heard not a sound, are you sure?

"Mrs. Krantz," Mrs. Mitchell scorned, "a mother knows when her child's needs are pressing. I suggest you not deride a young mother within the walls of her own home. Pretending you do not hear my struggles makes you no less haughty than a Yankee strolling Augusta."

"I do not wish to offend, but I merely heard no sounds from the baby—or you."

"I certainly know when a fellow gentlewoman brings snobbish tones upon me. I demand that you leave this instant!" Mrs. Mitchell growled.

Mrs. Krantz left the kitchen and strode toward the entrance. As she passed the small desk, she pressed a finger upon the folded post letter to reveal the remainder of the closing:

With deepest condolences,
James Carson
Lieutenant Colonel
Confederate States of America

Mrs. Krantz's departure was hastened upon reading these words and she secured the door behind her with a forceful pull. She scurried along the hall and down the back stairs to the alley entrance of the chemist.

LATER THAT EVENING, Mister and Mrs. Krantz met with Doctor Bray, an appointment the couple insisted was an urgent matter. Mrs. Krantz explained what she read in the letter from the army, and if the message preceding it was invariable, expressed her concern for the mental condition of Mrs. Mitchell.

"Surely she has gone mad with grief and pining and refuses to believe the truth laid out before her. Her complexion is visibly degraded and her constitution is suffering for certain. A woman in her condition is fully incapable of providing proper care to her own child if she cannot even care for herself!"

"Mrs. Krantz," Doctor Bray began, "have you seen anything that would bear witness to neglect toward the child? We mustn't jump without exhibit."

"None I have seen, but we must begin an investigation immediately if we shall properly intercept an undesirable situation. She will harm herself and the baby likewise!"

The doctor thought for a moment, then said, "I have not seen the baby since before Mister Mitchell left to fight. I will visit her on the morrow and insist I received a post from him with the request to check the health of his wholesome family."

The three agreed the plan laid before them was proper and well-intentioned.

• • •

THE NEXT DAY, Mrs. Mitchell stood in the window as the baby lay in its cradle. While she was watching two men load newly constructed long pine boxes onto a wagon, a muted tap came to her residence. Mrs. Mitchell hurried to the door and stated with soft assertion, "If this is Mister Krantz, you shall not be invited into my home again. If this is Mrs. Krantz, the same must be understood of you as well, with prominence!"

"Mrs. Mitchell, your visitor is Doctor Bray, I apologise if this is a time of inconvenience, but I have received a letter from your husband and would like to discuss my business with you."

"Doctor Bray, my apologies," she said as she opened the door, "Mister Krantz and his wife have been harassing me without reason and have made themselves unwelcome. Please come inside, but I must insist we keep our voices low, for the baby has just been laid to rest after a most difficult morning."

"Thank you, Mrs. Mitchell."

Doctor Bray stood next to the letter described by Mrs. Krantz the evening prior and with a quick glance could confirm the text she had recited.

"Doctor Bray, with what urgency do you pay me this visit?"

"I have received a post from your husband ..." he began.

Doctor Bray tapped his pockets in search of the letter about which he spoke to present Mrs. Mitchell, but found nothing.

"Alas, I seem to have left the correspondence in my medical office. Regardless, Mister Mitchell has written me and personally requested I visit his family and verify the health of his wholesome wife and budding baby."

"Oh thank you, Doctor Bray, my husband is of upstanding value and thinks only of the welfare of his family. I assure you we both are well and anticipate that very soon we shall be reunited with my loving husband."

"Of that, I have no doubts, Mrs. Mitchell. Being a man of upstanding value myself, I intend to write him back on the morrow and convey the wellness I have witnessed firsthand. But please, if you have no qualms, I must make notes on the objective state of my observations herein."

Doctor Bray proceeded with a standard inspection of health on Mrs. Mitchell and carefully noted his findings. He was not pleased to find that she was taking poor care of herself and had developed a concerning cough. Her weight was but a fraction of when he last visited the family before Mister Mitchell's departure. Dark pockets had formed around her sunken eyes and her skin wrinkled from dryness at every crease.

As was common for a keen physician, Doctor Bray inspected the living conditions of the patient with discretion and mentally noted an exaggerated lack of available food and drink. He noted the residence temperature to be very cold and several times he had to blow breath into his cupped palms for warmth.

But above all other concerns, Doctor Bray noted that he had not heard the baby fuss from its cradle since he had begun his visit.

"Mrs. Mitchell, I could not help but notice the peacefulness in which your baby sleeps. You have been blessed with a wonderful child of peace."

"Thank you, Doctor Bray, but not all times are as they are now. Many nights I pace my residence with the baby, comforting and caressing in hopes of peaceful slumber. Many mornings I pray for a break from the incessant wailing, a break from the noise and fog floating in my head. I pray for the day my husband will return and the baby will recognise him and smile and coo and babble. And once my husband rejuvenates his war-affected constitution with rest, at that time—and only that time—will I too rest."

Doctor Bray had not forgotten about the letter from the army, he had not forgotten the concerns of Mister and Mrs. Krantz—for his concerns were the same as theirs.

"Mrs. Mitchell, I'm certain once your husband returns, all will be well in your family. Please, in order for me to send Mister Mitchell my report, I ask of you to inspect the baby."

"Doctor Bray, I have spent so much time this morning before your arrival producing calm, I request we do not disturb the sleeping baby."

"Mrs. Mitchell, I understand your frustration, but with one quick check I can easily confirm your baby is healthy and vibrant and fruitful. Only then can I dictate my return correspondence with your husband to inform him of all things well."

Mrs. Mitchell brought her fingers to her chin as concern spread throughout her face.

"Please be careful, a tightly wrapped blanket makes all the difference for a baby to remain sleeping. It stimulates peace as when held tightly in their mother's loving arms."

Doctor Bray approached the cradle and observed the baby wrapped wholly in a soft blanket, one without enough bulk, perhaps, to provide proper warmth in the cold residence. This concerned Doctor Bray considering the noticed cough of Mrs. Mitchell.

Mrs. Mitchell moved to the window and formed a content smile as she watched two young boys collect pine cones on the grounds of the courthouse.

Doctor Bray brought his palm to the blanket covering the baby's legs and found no warmth emanating from within. He cupped his hands around the legs and discovered a much smaller child than his expectations.

"The baby is sleeping," Mrs. Mitchell assured as she observed one of the courthouse boys drop his full arms of pine cones to the ground.

Doctor Bray slid his hand inside the blanket to feel the baby's feet, discovered to be no larger than his own thumb and to be cold as a winter's day.

The boy with no pine cones ran to the other and pulled his

arms out of their embrace to cause all of his pine cones to fall as well. The first boy screamed at the other, "If mine have fallen, then yours shall be as well!"

Under the blanket, Doctor Bray slid his fingers up to the baby's thigh and found the temperature to match the cold of its feet.

"Mrs. Mitchell, do you not warm your residence in order to provide comfort for yourself and the baby?" Doctor Bray asked with his head turned to the lady.

"My condition is comfortable, I will not change it. And the baby only needs to get warmth while being held in the consuming love of a mother's arms. I am a good mother and my baby knows the comfort of my loving embrace."

The second boy grabbed the first at his waistcoat and thrust a fist onto the nose, a blow that caused sprawling limbs with a fall to the ground. Mrs. Mitchell smiled in amusement.

Doctor Bray brought his eyes back to the cradle and began to pull away the blanket from the baby's face. Revealed in slow, the baby's colour matched the blue hyacinths of Doctor Bray's garden in April.

Doctor Bray sprung to his feet, his face filled with horror.

"Good God!" he exclaimed.

Mrs. Mitchell rushed to the cradle and with haste covered the baby tightly into the blanket.

"Doctor Bray, your volume is too great! Please respect that the baby is sleeping!"

"But ... Mrs. Mitchell ... the baby ..." Doctor Bray stammered.

"I have given you full warning, good sir," Mrs. Mitchell said as she pointed to the door,

"I must insist you leave my residence promptly!"

"But I cannot ... the baby is ... is ..."

"Please vacate now!"

Mrs. Mitchell grabbed Doctor Bray by the arm and forced him into the hallway. She stretched out a pointed finger and held it near his throat.

"You are no longer welcome here, sir!"

She slammed the door upon his face and turned. Marching to the cradle, she lifted and held the baby firmly to her chest and rocked from side to side.

She knew the doctor's disruption to the baby's sleep would cause misfortune for her well into the night—this would certainly be another night of no sleep for both Mrs. Mitchell and the baby.

"Shhhhhh," she whispered over and over, "shhhhhh ..."

THE CHRISTMAS DEMON

O NCE UPON A TIME, the joyful decorations of Christmas celebration consisted of flowing ribbons of silver and gold, colors representing the brilliant heavens and the shining stars and the prayers of bringing good blessings to Earth.

In modern times, the traditional colors have become red and green; pine wreaths with big red bows, alternating candlesticks on windowsills, and hand-knit sweaters of dyed wool.

They say these are the colors of Christmas not because of any spiritual reference, but rather that these are the colors that keep the Christmas Demon away. It is lore that no one dares challenge, and lore, which to this day—it would seem, keeps them safe.

But I alone know the true history of this tradition, and the historical lore is whimsical nonsense to me. For I am the Christmas Demon and I return every year, every December, and those two colors certainly don't keep me away.

SINCE THE ORIGINS OF CHRISTMAS, I have existed. And every December thereafter, I have risen to Earth for three weeks to perform my deathly duties in the middle of the most joyous season for humans.

A demon's role is clearly defined: We shall appear in a glorious spectacle and make deals with the humans, deals which they will never be able to keep. Then they would be ours for the taking.

Regardless of how witty humans think they are, there are no challenges of intellect, nor tests of physical prowess that can defeat a demon. We are superior and we always win.

Some humans are outright greedy and simply want demons to bestow amazing skills upon them. Artists and musicians have always preferred this option. Some humans would make preposterous demands, then try to fool us with riddles. But we are the creators of all riddles, so this was just foolish of them.

BUT THEN I, THE CHRISTMAS DEMON, met a modest woman who was my undoing. I approached her on the first day of my arrival in a most glorious spectacle. I stood tall on my hooves, swept my tail with menace, and brought glow through my eyes. I informed her that she was whom I shall consume.

"But why you choose me?" she asked with honest humility, "You are a mighty demon, surely there are more impressive opponents to defeat."

I informed her that I choose whomever I wish, and she was the one I had chosen. She would have to make a deal with me. She thought for a minute, puzzled and focused, trying to formulate a challenge worthy of such a formidable opponent.

She resigned her thoughts and stated, "Demon, I have no idea how to defeat you. I take your presence as seriously as death itself, so I must ask you questions—with modesty—to help me understand you."

Her words were sincere as she continued, "Do you have hobbies—and which is your favorite?"

"My favorite hobby is defeating humans, of course! Humans are arrogant and cavalier and I love that these traits always lead to their undoing."

"Oh my goodness, I see."

She looked around at the wilted and dreary weather and said, "This dreadful weather is reminiscent of how you leave our village feeling after your departure, nothing like my beloved springtime joy. Demon, what is your favorite season?"

"Why, autumn of course! Autumn is the ushering in of death, and this—perhaps without surprise—is appealing to me," I responded with pride, "Autumn is the perfect precursor to my visit."

She thought for a few moments, absorbing my words to hopefully find something useful.

She probed further, "When the trees are changing in autumn, what is your favorite color of dying leaves?"

"A-ha!" I exclaimed, "I know how you are trying to trick me! Leaves don't change color—they remain the same year-round!"

I flexed my pointy fingers and hissed with satisfaction.

The woman paused in confusion, and responded, "And what color are these leaves, the leaves that don't change color?"

"They are gold, like my beautiful skin!" I stated. Then I stroked my face and wiggled my forked tongue in the most menacing way.

The woman pressed her lips tightly together and tilted her head back just the slightest, but said nothing.

I was growing impatient with her, "Woman, enough! I demand that you present your challenge so that we can make our deal in a timely manner."

After another lengthy pause, she spoke with slow confidence, "I have decided my challenge for you, demon. I will return in one hour and define the terms of the deal, then present my challenge. And finally, I will defeat you."

Since I am a demon, known to be superior to humans in every way, a mere delay of one hour was insignificant to me. I agreed and spent that time wisely tormenting children.

UPON HER RETURN, I WAS waiting.

"Begin!" I demanded.

"First, my terms," she said, "If you lose my challenge, you will be stripped of all your power to stake claims against humans, for all of time. Every December when you return, you will be powerless, Christmas Demon."

It didn't matter what terms she desired, for I would win. I always win.

"Agreed."

"Now for my challenge," she said. She held out a shallow burlap sack and spread the opening wide.

"A single one of these rose hip berries is ripe, the remaining ones are not. Choose the ripe berry, then eat it to validate your correctness."

"Ha!" I said with excitement, I have never had such an easy challenge. I looked into the bag and saw that all the berries were gold, which did not fool me. With all of my victories over the years, I have stolen berries from the tabletops of my victims and they have always been ripe and gold and delicious, so I knew that all of the berries in her sack were ripe. I chose a berry on top and held it high.

"You, woman, are mine," I snarled.

I placed the berry on my tongue and with my best intimidating sneer, bit down.

I had never experienced such horror to find this berry to be bitter and very much unripe. I spit it out and snarled, "Cheating a demon is grounds for immediate removal!"

I leaned into her face and bellowed my deepest and loudest growl.

But then she reached into the sack and picked up another of the berries.

"The ripe one, eat it to verify."

I snarled again and insisted that I would do no such thing.

She spoke with calm persistence, "Since I have already triumphed, you will need to convince yourself by eating this ripe berry."

"Woman, I will eat this berry and it will be unripe and I will take you. Your games are ridiculous."

I placed the berry on my tongue and with my best intimidating sneer, bit down. But this time the berry was ripe and fruity and delicious.

"How did you defeat me?" I thundered.

"You, demon, are color-blind. You cannot distinguish a green summer tree from a brilliant autumn one. You cannot tell that your own skin is a hideous shade of red. And you cannot tell a green unripe berry from a brilliant red ripe one. You, Christmas Demon, are now powerless."

THE WOMAN WENT ON TO CONVINCE others that in order to keep the Christmas Demon away, these two colors—red and green—should be on prominent display. Fearing the dark things they had seen the demon undertake in past years, the people adopted this change with wholehearted faith.

But it was, of course, not the real reason she spread such nonsense. It was her way of taunting me, for eternity, and pointing out the real consequences of being arrogant and cavalier. It was her way to remind me of a beauty within humans that I will never know—through colors I will never see. Her modesty stopped with me.

EVERY DECEMBER I RETURN still. But instead of harvesting humans, I spend all of my time hiding in shadows or walking alone through dark, empty fields. All of the humans have decorated for the season with abundant reds and greens, and, like every year, the Christmas Demon will not harm them.

For all of eternity, the Christmas Demon will not harm them.

TEN SHARP

TEN O'CLOCK IS APPROACHING and the band is about to start. It's in the contract—start at ten sharp or get docked pay for the night. As willing participants in a financially struggling art form, my jazz musicians always start on time.

When I asked for a job here twenty-five years ago, it was only to pay rent for the summer. Now, I'm proud to own this historic jazz club. It's where Capone's criminal underworld existed, literally, under our feet. The bootleg tunnels are still there but don't ask to see them. If you aren't replacing a Guinness keg, you don't go down there.

For the first several months, I was the bouncer—expressionless and unshakable as a bouncer should be. That's when I picked up the nickname Black Zeus. With my six-foot-five, three-hundred-pound frame and majestic beard, the resemblance was undeniable. Jazz clubs aren't known for riffraff, but having security in an establishment of alcohol and ego is pragmatic.

THE END OF THE BAR NEAREST the stage is missing a stool. I keep it tucked under the bar. Years ago, I applied a *RESERVED* sticker across the top. This particular stool only gets used by one special patron, one special girl.

Just before ten o'clock, just before the band counts off their first song, I bring it out.

The bands start at ten sharp—as per the contract—so that as she arrives, they've just begun swinging. She sits with ankles crossed and an elbow resting on the brown walnut bartop. She beams as the talented musicians enter their flow.

She always wears a smile. And sometimes laughs after a clever riff. Her applause is sincere.

THE DRUNK ARROGANT ONE from a group of Lincoln Park guys waves for my attention.

"What do you know about that girl?"

"Which one?" I rumble without looking.

"The one at the end of the bar," he says as he motions with his beer bottle.

"She loves jazz. More than anything, I'd guess."

He leans hard to catch another glimpse.

A patron near the window holds up two fingers. I touch the Guinness tap handle and he gestures a thumbs-up.

"What's she drinking?" the arrogant one asks.

I grab two empty pint glasses and initiate the first of two perfect pours.

"Nothing."

"Then send her a drink," he demands.

I raise one eyebrow, the only expression on the dark, chiseled face of Black Zeus.

"Send her a drink, my gargantuan friend!"

"You sure?"

"Yes, it's on me."

"She won't drink it."

"Why not?"

"She never drinks it."

Of all the drinks anyone has ever bought her, she's never touched a single one of them. Not once.

The arrogant one places a finger on his cheek and announces, "When I buy a girl a drink—just look at this face, she'll drink it."

"All right. Cash first."

"Put it on my tab."

"Nope. Her drink is cash first."

SHE ONLY STAYS ONE HOUR, so I don't have to waste too many drinks sent to her. When she leaves, at ten fifty-nine, I pull her stool and replace it back under the bar. It's always ten fifty-nine. And when she leaves, the scar on my bicep hurts—but only for a moment.

I remember the night I got this scar. It was the same night she died. She sat with ankles crossed and an elbow resting on the bartop, listening to her father play.

Back then, self-proclaimed cool cats flexed drama with delayed start times. But not the girl's father. He was so exuberant to be here that he started at ten sharp. He had almost reached an hour into his set when a drunken argument broke out at the stools. Before big Zeus could subdue the ruckus, two shots were fired—the first into my arm, the second into the girl.

Her father never performed here again, he stopped playing altogether after that night.

The girl started showing up about a month later. So I've seen her joy for many years—the pride of watching her father fulfill his dream still gives her glow.

IT WAS A SPECIAL NIGHT FOR HIM. He had been dreaming of performing here his whole life. Every day, for many years, he passed the club from behind the steering wheel of a tired CTA bus. Every day he'd give the club a wink. "I'm coming for ya," he'd say, "Be there soon."

It was a special night for the girl. It was her birthday. Her father had worked hard, and unselfishly, to raise his family over the years, and now he finally stood on the exact stage where all of his heroes had performed. As a gift to his daughter, he promised to play a new composition he wrote just for her, just for her birthday.

It was a special night for me, too. When the last note of the girl's song was held, and the applause slowed, her father planned to call her on stage. I was to follow her, drop to a knee, and pledge my undying love for her.

THE GIRL DOESN'T SHOW up all the time. It's never a particular day of the week. But when she comes, her stool is waiting. I always put it out, and that stool is reserved for her only.

And when she does arrive and take her seat, she will again glow with pride.

And I will smile at her joy, and admire her beauty.

And it will be ten sharp.

THE WORLD ENDS TODAY

———————

H AKIM SAT ON THE GRASS between the bus bench and the manicured base of a bent palm tree. He liked this spot. In the afternoons, as the peak heat of the day soaked into his dark skin, a condo building would stretch out its shadow and provide relief from the swelter. He didn't make much money sitting at this spot, but sometimes commuters would drop a few coins as they stood to enter the bus.

He never begged, he merely placed his plastic yellow can one arm's length in front of his crossed legs. The name of the instant coffee contents had long since faded, and now it merely read a hand-written, *Please*. One of Hakim's few possessions was a black marker, but it wasn't used too often.

He didn't like it when he saw others begging with a tattered piece of cardboard—one that professed their love of Jesus, lied about how many kids they had, or claimed the urgent need for a bus ticket to Detroit. Those others came and went, and moved on to new locations nearer the beach, but Hakim was steadfast to own the spot between the bus bench and the bent palm tree, marked with his yellow coffee can.

One day, as the fading sun tinted everything gold, a thin, elderly man approached and sat on the bench. He seemed preoccupied with worry that he would be late for something. He stood and stretched his neck to look down the street, the bus should be along soon. He sat and fidgeted with his watch. He squinted at the sky as if the condo was a compass and he could determine the time by the fall of its shadow.

Hakim had made a sign earlier that day, on the way to his spot. He found a fresh piece of cardboard behind the grocery market, cleanly cut from the lid of a produce box. His writing was shaky, but the text was clear, *The World Ends Today.*

The man on the bench noticed the sign, and mumbled under his breath, "The world ends today ... nonsense, no it doesn't."

Hakim, a man of modesty and few words, heard this and tilted his head.

"It does for me."

The man stood from the bench and craned his neck looking for the bus.

"Ridiculous. Where is that—I'm starving."

His fidgeting eyes stopped moving and locked focus on the fast-food chicken restaurant across the street.

"12-piece bucket for $5.99?"

He closed his eyes and breathed in the aromatic, chicken-grease air.

"Mmmm. Smells so good."

The man did a double-take look at Hakim, then outstretched his arm and pointed at the restaurant.

"Is that place any good?"

"Haven't had any for a while," Hakim said with a shrug.

"I see. But the last time you had it, was it any good?

After a series of slow nods, Hakim said, "Very."

The man stood and craned his neck down the street as he said, "Stupid bus."

With a frustrated sigh, he walked to the stoplight and crossed the street to enter the restaurant.

Hakim didn't give this interaction much thought, but he

did notice that the bus rumbled past while the man was in the restaurant.

THE OLD MAN RETURNED to the bench with a large sack bearing the restaurant's logo.

"I hope you're right," he said to Hakim.

He looked at his watch, thought for a moment, then raised one hand in the air.

"Argh, that was the last express bus," he exclaimed.

Hakim lifted his eyes.

The man looked down the street, then the other way, then turned toward the bench and placed his restaurant sack down on the seat.

"That's it, I'm eating right here," he said.

He bent over and removed a large paper bucket of chicken and placed it on the bench. With a simple tug, the lid popped off. He lifted the bucket to his face and took a deep breath.

"Wonderful," he said.

He removed a plate from the sack and transferred three pieces of chicken to it. He stopped and stared at it for a moment before moving his eyes to Hakim, who was still watching him.

"What's your name?" the man said.

"Hakim."

"Well, Hakim, since you suggested this place, I don't see why I can't pay you back. I'm not *that* much of a soulless wretch."

He carried the plate to Hakim, who after a brief hesitation, welcomed the offer.

"Thank you," Hakim said, "it's been a long time."

The old man stepped back to the bench and prepared his own plate with three pieces.

"Long time for what?" he finally asked.

Hakim's mouth was full, so he mumbled, "I dunno."

The old man took a bite and hummed with satisfaction.

"Hakim, my friend, you were correct. Delicious."

They both ate in silence for several minutes. At one point, the man reached into the sack and grabbed a bottle of water. He loosened the top, then replaced it. Stepping over to Hakim, he handed him the water. Hakim looked but didn't reach for it.

"Go on, take it. I have another."

Hakim looked at the sack, then back at the man, then took the water.

"Thank you," he mumbled.

"I thought you might want one, so I bought two."

The old man opened his own water and they both drank.

"You know," the man said, "I don't like your sign. At all. Why do you think the world ends today?"

Hakim took pause and rested his forearms on his knees. He squinted and looked down the street, at nothing in particular.

"Thank you for being nice to me, for the chicken, but I've lost the will to live. I've decided today will be my last one."

The old man placed one hand on his hip and tilted his head with concern. His other hand held a chicken leg, which he used to motion toward Hakim.

"I see, lost the will to live."

He squinted and blinked a few times as he looked up at the condo balconies. He began to smile, then broke into deep laughter.

"I'm sorry you think it's funny," Hakim said.

"No, no. I'm not laughing at you. I just remembered something," the old man said.

He rubbed his forehead and laughed again.

"There was this kid I knew growing up, everyone called him *Will-to-Live*. That guy was such a daredevil. Man, did he drink in every single drop of life he could."

The man paused and took a deep breath behind his smile.

"Will-to-Live, nothing he wouldn't try once. I grew up in San Francisco, and boy are there some steep hills. This one time, Will-to-Live took a few of us over to his aunt's neighborhood, rode our bikes over to Castro and … Alvarado—I'm pretty sure—yeah."

"All right, you mugs," Will-to-Live barked out, "all the way down with no brakes. Feet off the pedals, put 'em on the front fork. Everyone got it?"

The kids looked at each other. Totally scared to death. Then they nodded.

Will-to-Live moved his pointed finger across the other boys.

"Got it? No brakes 'til you pass 24th. Ready?"

Everyone squeezed their handgrips and lifted one foot to a pedal for that first push.

"And remember … don't die."

Will-to-Live flashed that cocky smile and went first.

Here we are, picking up ridiculous speed down that hill, and—now I remember, that's right, the last kid to go was the little guy, we called him Lil' B—real name was Benny something, but he was so tiny, how could we not call him that.

Years later Lil' B told us what he was thinking about up on Castro that day, as he watched the other kids pick up speed in front of him. It wasn't about crashing or dying, but about the time he got in trouble at school.

He sassed back to the teacher—and I'm sure she deserved it.

Anyway, he was sitting in the principal's office, all tiny in that chair, watching Mister Oaks pace back and forth and scold him about keeping quiet in class. A knock came on the door and Mister Oaks stepped out into the front office.

Lil' B is just sitting there, waiting, when he hears Will-to-Live whispering from outside the open window, "Pssst, Lil' B, come here!"

Now, it's important to know that Mister Oaks' office is on the second floor—how in the world could Will-to-Live be outside the window?

Lil' B hurries over to the window and peeks out to find Will-to-Live had climbed a drain pipe and was listening the whole time. He had a cigarette hanging out his mouth and a big smile.

"Hey B!" he said with that cocky smile.

"Get out of here, he'll bust you!" Lil' B warned.

"All right, all right. But first—"

Will-to-Live grips the pipe tighter with one arm and pulls the cigarette out of his mouth. He hands that thing to Lil' B.

"Drag it, man!"

Lil' B grabs the cigarette and takes a puff before darting back to his seat.

"Copacetic!" Will-to-Live said with a big nod, "Good luck, Lil' B!"

Just then Mister Oaks comes back in and sits at his desk.

"I think we're about done here with—" he began.

He stopped himself and turned his head to the side.

"Do you smell smoke?"

And Lil' B, that kid could keep a straight face lemme tell ya, he looks Mister Oaks square in the eye and says, "I do. Have you been smoking, Mister Oaks? I don't think that's allowed on school property."

That little comment cost him a week of detention. Boy, did he earn our respect from that one.

So Lil' B is about to race down Castro and that's what he's thinking about—the time Will-to-Live snuck him a cigarette in Mister Oaks' office. That was his life-flashing-before-your-eyes moment.

Man, were we hauling ass! Full-speed, we're about to launch through Elizabeth street ...

The man paused his story to find the bus pulling up to the stop.

"Well, Hakim, I gotta go," he said.

Hakim had stopped eating and his mouth was hanging open. The man handed the bucket with the remaining chicken to Hakim.

"Enjoy."

The man stepped onto the bus and the doors closed. Hakim watched as the bus pulled away through the intersection.

Hakim lowered his eyes to the bucket of chicken. After a few moments, he looked back to find the bus turning the corner two stoplights down.

· · ·

THE NEXT DAY, AT THE SAME time, the old man arrived at the bench and sat. He fidgeted with his watch, then stood to look for the bus. He remembered the events of the day before and turned to Hakim's spot. Hakim was there. He was sitting with legs crossed, the yellow can resting in its previous spot, and again, was holding the sign, *The World Ends Today*.

Hakim had noticed the man arrive, but said nothing and kept his eyes down. The old man stared at Hakim until Hakim finally returned the glance. The man broke eye contact, then checked his watch and looked for the bus. Turning back to Hakim, he found him still watching.

"Hello, Hakim," the old man said, "I see you're not dead."

Hakim said nothing.

The man checked his watch, looked down the street, then left the bench to repeat his chicken run from the day before.

And again, the last express bus rumbled past without stopping.

THE MAN RETURNED WITH a large sack bearing the restaurant's logo. He set it on the bench and turned to Hakim.

"You got me hooked on this chicken."

He opened the bucket and placed three pieces of chicken, and now a biscuit, on a paper plate. He picked up a water bottle and walked over to Hakim. Bending over, he waved the plate under Hakim's nose before lowering it to his hands. Hakim took the plate, looked up at the man, and nodded.

"Thank you," Hakim said.

"Don't forget your water. It's not a pretty sight when someone chokes to death on their food."

The old man held out the water. Hakim nodded again and took the bottle.

The man stepped back to the bench to load up his own plate. When finished, he sat.

"Thought I'd try the biscuits today. Looked good."

They ate for a while in silence, the old man occasionally humming with satisfaction.

"I HUNG OUT WITH WILL-TO-LIVE quite a bit growing up," the man said.

Hakim lifted his eyes from his plate to listen.

"One Halloween, when we were teenagers, some of us packed into a car and drove down to Palo Alto. Will-to-Live had just learned about TP-ing houses, and he was ready to try it out. We tooled around a bit near the frat houses until we spotted a big house with a gigantic party. Perfect.

"We parked a block away and everyone grabbed rolls of toilet paper from the trunk. We snuck over to that house and began throwing the rolls into the trees. Up … down, streaming trails of white flowing in the wind. It was beautiful.

"We were nearly done when this huge mountain of a guy stepped onto the porch and spotted us. He dropped his beer and yelled into the house. I don't know what he said, but his voice was deep and it was loud. And that animalistic call meant something to everyone in the house because there was soon a bunch of guys flowing out of that house.

"Turns out we had chosen the house where all of the Stanford football players were partying. And the thing about football players is, is that they're big, and they're fast. We took off running, but none of us were athletes, so that really sucked. A few of us hid in bushes—two more slid underneath cars, but me and Will-to-Live, we ran like our asses were on fire.

"Did I mention that football players are fast? No matter what we did, they kept getting closer. We ran down an alley next to a church and Will-to-Live grabbed a door handle and we zipped inside. We braced the door and could hear them running past outside, whooping and hollering.

"Did I mention that we weren't athletes? Our hearts were pounding so hard, man, we thought that was the end of us. Gasping for air, sweating, bent over in exhaustion."

THE OLD MAN PAUSED AND TOOK a big drink of his water as if he had just run into that church. Hakim was so enthralled by the story, the chicken between his hands had not yet been bitten.

"So there we are, near death, hiding in a church on Halloween. Next thing we know, there's a priest standing in front of us, black robe, white collar. And he's somewhere between confused and scared."

"Are you boys all right?" the priest asked.

Will-to-Live placed his palms together and responded like he had been rehearsing it all night.

"Yes, Father, thank you. We ran here as fast as we could to attend tonight's mass. I'm so sorry we're late."

And do you know what that priest said?

THE OLD MAN HEARD THE BUS approaching. He picked up the bucket and handed it to Hakim.

"This is me," the man said.

He stepped up into the bus and the doors closed. Hakim watched with wide eyes as the bus pulled away and headed to the second stoplight.

• • •

THE NEXT DAY, AT NEARLY THE SAME time, the old man arrived at the bench. But he had already stopped at the restaurant and was carrying the big sack with the restaurant logo on it.

Hakim was in his usual spot, as was his yellow can. His prophetic sign was laying on the ground next to him.

The man set the food on the bench and prepared a plate for Hakim.

"Hakim, I have a daughter. Do you have any children?" the man asked as he handed the plate to Hakim.

"Yes. I have two sons."

"My daughter and I had a rough patch for a few years, a while back."

The man prepared his own plate and sat on the bench.

"She was going through her teens and was embarrassed by her old man—by everything I did. I was a good provider for the family, took care of everyone, bought her the things she wanted. Started my own business, too. But even that was a big embarrassment to her."

The man held up a biscuit and inspected it.

"But it didn't matter, she was going through a phase, and she just didn't like anything I did. She was gone from my life for a while."

He peeled off the crispy bottom layer of the biscuit and ate it.

"The only thing I could do was wait. Wait for her to realize, wait for her to come back, and hope she regretted her past. Between you and me, I didn't want to be around her if she didn't."

Hakim removed the lid from his water bottle and held it near his lips, but tipped it away before he drank.

"What happened?" he asked.

The old man nodded and wiped his mouth with a napkin.

"She found peace with herself. She visited me one day and apologized. We both cried and we laughed and we caught up on each other's lives. It was nice."

Hakim had stopped eating and was looking down with great sadness. He pursed his lips and nodded.

"Thank you," he said.

THE OLD MAN VISITED HAKIM EVERY day for three weeks. He told half-finished stories of his adventures with Will-to-Live. He talked about the difficulties of starting a small business while having a family, and how satisfying it was. He talked about his love for roller coasters. And he talked about the excitement he had for the future.

Hakim had started sitting on the bench to dine alongside his new friend. At one point, the old man had given Hakim a stack of gift certificates for free chicken at the restaurant.

"I made friends inside since you've been sending me there every day," the man said with a wink.

Hakim kept them in his pocket, unnecessary since the man arrived with food every day.

The man never asked Hakim about how or why he ended up on the grass under the bent palm tree. He never preached to Hakim and he never made him feel bad. He did, however, make him smile a few times.

• • •

ONE DAY, THE OLD MAN DIDN'T show up. Hakim waited long after the sun went down until he left for the shelter. He arrived too late to get a bed for the night. He sat outside on the sidewalk, staying awake through sunrise, thinking about the old man, thinking about his sons, and thinking about Will-to-Live.

As the day crept on, and *Chicken Time*—as the old man had named it—rumbled past, he again didn't show up. But then a middle-aged woman came and sat on the bench, checking her watch over and over. Hakim had been watching her. But, as usual, said nothing.

At one point she stood to leave, but her feet didn't move. She took a deep breath and turned to Hakim.

"Mister Hakim?" she said, as more of a statement than a question.

"Yes?"

"My father passed away yesterday. I'm afraid he won't be coming by anymore."

Hakim felt a sad warmth creep through his chest and neck.

"How?" he asked.

"He was at the end of a very long battle with cancer."

"I'm sorry, I didn't know," he said, his voice beginning to tremble.

The woman wiped away a tear.

"Thank you ..." she said, "for giving him joy these past few weeks."

"I did nothing," Hakim pondered, "I just sat."

"Yes, I know. You just sat ... and listened. And let him relive his youth and his adventures, and bathe in his unbounded will to live. Even in the end, he just couldn't seem to give up. So ... thank you."

"It was my pleasure, I assure you."

Hakim stood and brushed off his pants. He picked up his sign and tucked it under his arm. He lifted his yellow can and turned to walk away, but hesitated.

"Ma'am? I consider your father my friend. But he never told me his name or where he was always going in such a hurry."

"His name is William. And I'm not sure where he *pretended* to be going because he lived right here," she said as she pointed to the condo building, "overlooking the chicken restaurant he founded."

Hakim lowered his head and closed his eyes. He stood motionless, then nodded.

"Thank you," he said in a soft voice, "Thank you both."

"Hakim?" the woman said.

He turned to face her.

"Yes, ma'am?"

"Where are you going?"

Hakim squinted through his tears and looked down the street, at nothing in particular.

He lifted his sign to inspect its message, *The World Ends Today*. He smiled as he tore it in half.

"I have two sons. It's time to apologize to them."

· ·

PLIGHT OF THE ARTIST

A tender dream insistent
Umbra to eye's glimmer
The shadow more persistent
Fleeting is the shimmer

ACKNOWLEDGMENTS

This book is the culmination of three long years of work; the journey from first idea seed to a physical book in hand has been both challenging and rewarding. I'd like to recognize the fine folks at Titan Shore Press for their encouragement, attention to detail, and endless patience.

A few of these stories started out as ideas for short film screenplays that were destined to never see the light of day. Special thanks to the team at Saturn Moon Beach for parting with their narratives so that they could be given new life in this collection of short-form fiction.

A special acknowledgment goes out to Elise Tran for her invaluable editorial contributions and feedback during development. Because of her amazing talent and generosity, my voice is stronger and my writing will forever jump higher off the page.

ABOUT THE AUTHOR

PATRICK SEDA was born in eastern Iowa and raised in Chicago. He studied engineering and medicine at the University of Iowa and is a graduate of the Biomedical Engineering program. Along with writing fictional prose and poetry, he is a screenwriter and filmmaker. He is also a film screener for multiple international film festivals. Patrick currently resides in Atlanta.